The Collector

by

Mathias G. B. Colwell

F & I
by Melange Books

Published by
Fire and Ice
A Young Adult Imprint of Melange Books, LLC
White Bear Lake, MN 55110
www.fireandiceya.com

The Collector ~ Copyright © 2013 by Mathias G. B. Colwell

ISBN: 978-1-61235-774-4 Print

Names, characters, and incidents depicted in this book are products of the author's imagination or are used fictitiously. Any resemblance to actual events, locales, organizations, or persons, living or dead, is entirely coincidental and beyond the intent of the author or the publisher. No part of this book may be reproduced or transmitted in any form or by any means, electronic or mechanical, including photocopying, recording, or by any information storage and retrieval system, without permission in writing from the publisher.
Published in the United States of America.

Cover Art by Becca Barnes

The Collector
Mathias G. B. Colwell

The world was nearly consumed by chaos and madness during The Great Transformation, a time when myth and legend were given form overnight. Nearly half a century later, The Collectors Guild, a sect of humans tasked to search and control the supernatural, are still trying to clean up the mess that was made of society. Vampires, werewolves and so much more come to life in this darkly gripping tale of love, friendship, betrayal, and most of all freedom.

I would like to dedicate this book to my parents. Your continual support and belief in me has made not only this dream, but all my dreams possible. Thank you.

Chapter One

A knife thudded into the wooden doorframe near his head just as Philip started to peer around the corner. Coattails swirled behind the knife thrower as he ducked into the next room. Watching the weapon quiver from impact so close to his head, he told himself he'd be more careful next time. If that was ever possible! Ripping the blade out of the wood, he hefted it in the palm of his hand before following the youth inside, ducking instinctively at the low ceiling. This dingy apartment was not unlike the usual places where he pursued riffraff. He'd seen places like it hundreds of times.

As he moved inside he traded the foul night air, smelling of refuse and chamber pots emptied from second story windows, for a somewhat different, but no less abhorrent, scent of spoiled food and stale sweat. Philip paced quickly across what was a barren living room and followed the lad through the next doorway.

The skinny youth stood at the other end of a hallway. The lad called out with an odd grin and dangerous glint in his eye, "I'd stop right there if I was you, that first knife was just a warning. The next one I throw will be far more deadly." He wore a mismatched set of clothing with a mess of necklaces and bracelets of all varieties. His faded red tunic, although it had once been bright, now bore the marks of greasy fingerprints. The tight fitting velvet coat appeared a decade or two out of style, flaring out slightly over narrow black trousers. A hooknose and thin features were sheltered, under a shock of unkempt brown hair. All in all, a typical gypsy lad, come to America from the Isles. Only he must be so much more since Philip had orders to bring him in.

Philip raised his hands in a peaceful gesture and didn't make a move down the hall towards his prey. "I just want to talk." The lie rang as false on his lips as it sounded in his head.

The young man threw back his head fearlessly and laughed in derision, then spoke in what sounded like an Irish brogue. "You Collectors never want to just talk. Your definition o' talk always comes with a heavy price and we both know that's the truth." It was true. As much as Philip wished it were not, talking to his quarries just never seemed to accomplish anything. Besides, by the time he was pursuing them, they'd almost always crossed a line too far past the restrictions of society to make talking even an option.

"Surrender quietly and it'll go much easier on you." Philip patted the small cord of rope coiled on his belt as he abandoned the ruse of wanting to talk to the lad. "There are no windows in this piece of dirt apartment and there's no back door. You're trapped." He tried to make his voice sound more reasonable, less harsh.

His foe laughed again. "You think that rope can hold me?"

"It will if I feed you some Nightsleep." Philip patted a small jar of the sleep-inducing substance he kept holstered on his other hip. For the first time Philip saw a flicker of fear dance across the lad's eyes. But quick as it had been there it was gone, with only a smirking face left in its wake. The kid was brave and confident. It would be wise to go carefully at this one since his abilities were somewhat of an unknown.

The youth began advancing slowly down the hall towards Philip. "We both know I'm not coming in peacefully, so let's drop the charade." All trace of friendliness had vanished from his face and only a focused expression remained. Without warning, he rushed along the narrow corridor toward Philip in a clatter of bracelets, necklaces, and earrings. The lad was fast! Philip tucked the extra knife he'd just acquired behind his belt and made ready for a take-down.

The youth dodged one way then the other, quick as lightning, and tried to squirm his way between Philip's right side and the wall. Philip jerked his right arm up in a clothesline action and knocked the lad clean off his feet with one blow. He took a step back as the gypsy-boy popped back up, wiping blood from the corner of his mouth and looking at Philip with a newfound respect.

The Collector

A fight appeared inevitable and Philip cracked his knuckles in his best menacing fashion. Unphased, the youth rushed him again, this time whipping out a new knife from somewhere on his body, and slashed left and right with swift, sure movements.

Philip leaned from side to side, trying to avoid the blade, and then swung his fist. When his opponent ducked, Philip's hand went through the wall to his left leaving splinters on the floor as he ripped it back out. Gasping, Philip realized his chest and shoulder were bleeding from a few shallow nicks. He could see the blood dripping from the knife as his opponent danced out of the way of Philip's fists.

The fellow's eyes were bright with battle, and Philip knew his type, the kind that got a feverish excitement from the heat of conflict. Philip wasn't immune to this sensation himself; he'd been in enough fights to feel the rush of blood to the head. Not an altogether unpleasant sensation.

But he had no more time to think as the fight blurred thick and fast. The youth pulled a third knife, which had been hidden in some part of his apparel, and forced Philip to yank out his own knife to deprive his opponent of an advantage. He preferred fighting with his fists whenever possible but that wasn't always a good idea. Some situations called for different tactics.

Blade clashed on blade as the boy danced in close and slashed again, leaving a slightly deeper gash on Philip's left thigh and sending a thin flow of blood onto his brown, form-fitting trousers. But for all his dazzling speed, the lad had underestimated Philip's strength. The Collector finally landed a massive blow to the lad's chest and sent him sliding back ten feet along the dusty wood floor as he fell.

In this pause, like the eye of the storm, he watched warily as the gypsy picked himself up yet again, appearing only a bit dazed from the impact of Philip's fist, yet nonetheless not too worse for wear after receiving such a blow. He grinned again, with a look that implied some hidden knowledge, as if he had just been toying with his opponent.

"You're stronger than ya' look, Collector." He whistled a catchy little tune, waiting for Philip to close the distance between them, "but I'm faster than you are strong."

Then, with an unfathomable burst of speed, he feinted one way before wriggling under Philip's attempt to collar him and racing down the hallway into the living room and out into the dark night beyond.

Calling out a parting taunt, "Best o'luck next time!" he disappeared, leaving only the jangle of his trinkets. Philip followed out of the apartment, more out of principle than any real hope of catching his quarry. He saw no one, only the dark street. Where was Philip's partner with the wagon when he needed him? These wounds, although none grave, required tending. He considered searching again for the lad but reasoned it would most likely just be fruitless wandering. Instead, Philip made his way back to the port where he could take care of his wounds on their ship and catch a wink of sleep on one of the hammocks before the morning came, instead of being left to fulfill his duties without a night's sleep.

The streets of New York City passed uneventful as he strode purposefully towards the wharf. At times his boots thudded on cobblestones, but other streets were hardly more than mud in this winter weather and left his calf-high black boots caked and brown. His trousers and even his pale linen shirt tucked loosely into his trousers became speckled with dirt.

He'd opted to leave his coat behind at the start of the night, preferring freedom and mobility in a fight, to the added restriction a coat would offer. He had begun to regret that decision by the time he reached his ship. The wind whipped forcefully around some corners and not at others as if nature herself couldn't decide upon her mood.

Upon reaching his destination, Philip went aboard silently, as was habit for a Collector. Once on deck, he made his way to the ship's small medical closet and gathered the materials needed to stitch up the shallow knife wounds he bore from the fight. He sewed himself up as deftly as possible for a man whose only experience with a needle and thread was in situations such as this. When he finished, the cuts had closed and would stay that way as he wound bandages around the stitches.

It was time for some rest. Thankful to have left the windy city streets behind, he strode across the deck. The wind seemed to die down enough that by the time Philip made his way into the hammock, the

The Collector

creaking of his ship and those around him provided only the normal amount of noise created by sailing vessels rocking gently on a night tide.

Philip fell asleep almost immediately. Yet it felt like he awakened quickly when morning's dull grey light fluttered across his eyelids. He opened his eyes, and thought of closing them again only for the briefest of moments before the rumbling of his stomach won out over the gritty feeling under his eyelids.

Philip rolled out of the hammock, for once grateful that he didn't have to pull on his clothes and boots since he hadn't disrobed at all when he went to bed. He stomped down to the galley to grab a bite for breakfast. As he entered, the ship's cook greeted him with a scowl, pointing out that all they had for breakfast was porridge and milk. "If I had more money, I could buy us some fresh provisions instead of having to live off these army rations you force me to use," the cook complained in a tired voice. It appeared someone else might not have had a full night's sleep either.

The man always griped about the lack of resources. However, food didn't matter much to Philip. He was a plain man, with plain tastes. If the offering filled his belly, it was good enough for him, and he wasn't about to spend extravagantly on unnecessary supplies when more necessary items cost so dear. Holding some of his prey often required a variety of concoctions and the herbs needed for those substances were not always common. Many apothecaries and herb women around the country would charge a man an arm and a leg to procure them.

Philip finished his meal quickly and in silence, and then decided to inspect his cargo holds. Their departure had been scheduled for today, if all went according to plan, and he wanted to make certain that everything was in order.

The ship's timbers creaked eerily as the vessel swayed on the morning tide. The Salt-Spray was a solid ship, built to withstand the transatlantic passage, as she'd done so many times in the ten years Phillip had owned her. The upper cargo area was packed with merchandise to be sold as a front for his occupation in London, Liverpool, or wherever he desired. He descended all the way down the last ladder. Here in the deepest hold in the belly of the ship, he carried an altogether different cargo than your typical merchandise.

A voice, cracked and thin with age, cackled hysterically in the cage to his left, setting off a chorus of grunts and whistles from the wooden box to his right. He turned to the person in the cage and shook his head warningly.

"It will go better for you if you stay silent," he cautioned sternly. The face that before had mirrored madness now contorted into a malevolent mask of rage. It was a different kind of madness he supposed, and he couldn't blame the thing's emotions. *Person*, he reminded himself. She was a person. Twenty-five years officially in the guild, and a childhood spent learning its every rule and protocol, yet Philip promised himself that he wouldn't forget that his quarries were still human. Well, some of them at least. He would never let himself become so indoctrinated into the system that he couldn't hold onto that one shred of decency in a line of work that was either dangerous, dirty, or downright depressing. The witch's eyes took on a shade of red, as the blood rushed to her face, and she tried to mutter an incantation through the muzzle covering her mouth. Philip blinked and then stared steadily at her as she attempted futilely to summon to memory the simple phrase that could free her.

"I wouldn't do that if I were you," he warned. "The mixture of Brainstone and fennel I feed you every morning and night prevents your mind from being able to process thoughts and produce sentences." He shrugged. "If you try to force yourself, you'll only rupture blood vessels in that tired old head of yours, and if too many burst I don't think I'll be able to save you."

The haggard old lady snorted and jerked her head backwards, as if she somehow thought that by doing so she would be able to free herself from the muzzle that prevented her from opening her mouth more than a crack. It covered the lower half of her face, complimenting the stringy, once-white, hair that hung limply to the sides of her head. All of her thrashing wore her out and her body slumped back against the wooden chair to which she was chained. The chair was nailed to the ground so all of her efforts had availed her not a single sentence, nor one inch of shift in her circumstances.

Philip should have felt pleased; she was a threat after all. A vicious killer, and user of men and women alike, the kind of subject that once

The Collector

apprehended, was best when locked away in the deepest vault at St. Thomas's. He knew it was truth, but sometimes it was hard to see the look in their eyes when he carted them away. He and his partner had collected her in Massachusetts nearly two weeks ago, before sailing south, and she was definitely one of their more dangerous acquisitions. He watched a moment more to make sure she was truly mollified. Satisfied that the witch was sufficiently subdued, he turned and made his way back along the narrow aisle that was created by the various boxes, cages and contrivances for keeping things contained that held the rest of his cargo.

He held the lantern aloft as high above his head as he could, illuminating only a fraction of the hold around him. Outside the air would be sharp and wintery, with possibly a fresh morning breeze to waft the smell of fish, unwashed sailors, and the salt and brine of the sea across a person's nose. Compared to the aromas that assailed his nostrils down here, the thought of outside air was a veritable luxury. Bodily waste and urine mixed with the smell of bilge, blood, and strangely even the scent of a swamp, formed a pungent odor, worse than any he had ever imagined. Well, until he had joined the guild that is. After his first assignment he had rather quickly rethought all of his romanticized versions of the career he had chosen. Falling into a Changeling's latrine would do that to you.

The orange glow his light source emitted illuminated boxes briefly as he strode by them, working his way through the maze of crates towards the ladder entrance from the primary hold above him. He wormed his way past a particularly wobbly coffin that was propped up against a large box to his left, as he turned the corner into the few yards of open space surrounding the ladder. He lowered the lantern as he twisted his body to turn, and then he brought it back up to shine on the open area as he continued on his way. As the light came up, he found himself face to face with a snarling mouth. The attack was instantaneous.

Hands closed about his throat and squeezed to kill. He jammed his own fingers into the eyes and neck of his assailant in an attempt to keep him at bay. The creature flexed powerful muscles and flung him against the wall of the cargo hold. Philip crashed to the floor with a painful thud and struggled up to his hands and knees only for the thing to fling itself upon him once more. It landed upon him, a mass of dirty skin, ragged, and torn clothes, and the smell of unwashed blood. This time it was Philip's turn to grasp his attacker's throat and hold the thing at bay. Saliva dripped onto his face as the thing closed in, straining for a bite of his flesh with blackened human teeth.

Philip recognized the half-man as one of his nastier captives. Leaning towards him, it forced its mouth a mere inch or so from his face before Philip remembered the silver dagger he kept at his waist. He risked letting go of the beast with his right hand to snatch the knife out of his belt and then brought it up with vicious speed into his opponent's side. His thrust was not a killing blow, but the thing gave an anguished howl until Philip smashed his left hand into its face and sent it twitching to the floor.

Not many creatures could match Philip for strength and it had been some time since he'd been so hard pressed to defend himself. It did not surprise him, however, every guild member knew that a werewolf's first and most well planned assault was accompanied by an extreme rush of strength, even one that was still in human form due to it not being a full moon.

One of the well-documented characteristics of a werewolf. If you were strong enough to fight it off and resist that first onslaught as he had just now, then its following attempts weakened until you either defeated it or it ran off. Assuming, however, you were strong enough to fend off even a less than full power werewolf. It wasn't as easy as it sounded. Luckily, Philip had a physical trait of his own that not many people knew about. The thing, *the man*, he reminded himself yet again, lay unconscious from his final blow. It wouldn't stay that way for long.

Philip realized that the trap door above his head was open, and he glanced up into the wide-eyed stare of a twelve-year-old boy looking down at him. Philip grunted as he pushed himself up from the ground and grabbed the ankle of the werewolf and began dragging it back towards its confinement.

"Stephen, come down here," he commanded the boy in a quiet but authoritative tone.

The boy gulped and proceeded to shuffle his way down the ladder from one hold to the next. "Yes, sir?"

The Collector

Philip almost snorted at the boy's attempt at innocence. He would have if he had not just found himself in such a precarious situation. Lucky his mouth had been closed and none of the werewolf's saliva had found its way inside, otherwise things might have been far worse. He doubted that the venom would have changed his physical form, as his own biological quirks would probably nullify that mutation, but he still might have become a carrier, capable of infecting others. Carriers sometimes became more dangerous than the real thing since they often had no idea they might be transmitting the curse even through the simplest of interactions such as a kiss.

"How many times have I told you to check all of the cages while I am out on a night's mission?" He fought for patience he didn't feel. "Is being a guild apprentice important to you or not? You must pay attention to details."

The boy dropped his head and muttered, "Yes, sir."

"How did the beast escape?" Philip already had an idea how, but it didn't hurt to let the boy find his own way to the proper conclusions.

Stephen squirmed uncomfortably. "I don't know, sir."

"Guess then, if you have not a clue," Philip retorted, keeping his exasperation as far from his voice as possible, and repeating over and over to himself that all was well that ended well, and nothing had come of this latest lapse in the boy's attention to detail.

"Well, sir," the boy answered in the accent he had acquired on the rough alleys of London's backstreets, "I suppose, if I had to speculate, there might possibly have been something I did wrong…" he trailed off.

Philip shook his head, his patience nearly at an end. "Just answer the question truthfully, you're not in too much trouble. Yet."

Stephen steeled himself and appeared to finally give up his worthless attempt to hide the truth. "I must have forgotten to douse his chains in the Wolfsbane water last night," he muttered in embarrassment.

Philip patted the boy on the shoulder before turning a corner in the cargo hold as he hauled the captive back along one of the aisles toward its cage. "There, Stephen, was that so hard to answer me plainly?"

The boy seemed encouraged that his overseer didn't appear too angry, and so he shook his head in relief.

"But how many times have I told you that you must take extra care to monitor our captives with the most extreme caution? This is the biggest load we have ever taken, and another unfortunate occurrence such as this could have disastrous consequences." Philip shuddered inwardly to imagine what might happen should a creature break loose and decide to free its fellow captives. He inclined his head at Stephen and raised his furry eyebrows, trying to instill a mite of worry into his apprentice. "You do know that this werewolf isn't even the most dangerous thing we're carrying, don't you?"

"Yes, Master Philip," Stephen responded in the meekest of tones.

Philip dragged the body behind him and proceeded to test the boy. "What is the best way to keep a werewolf confined?" He stared directly at Stephen, his face demanding an answer.

"A cage made of pure silver, of course, sir," the boy fired back.

"And if one isn't available?" he followed up just as quickly. Silver cages were rarely used due to difficultly in procuring them. The Guild had access to the treasuries of many governments, but still, an entire silver cage would cost a fortune. Not many people were willing to go to that length when there were other ways to keep a werewolf locked up.

The lad answered promptly yet again. "Exactly what we are doing, or supposed to be doing." He eyed the body they were hauling back to its cage a bit apprehensively; as if still unsure he wouldn't be punished for his failure to comply with caging regulations from their guild-provided handbook. "Chains doused morning and night in Wolfsbane water, is enough to hold the creature fast."

Philip nodded his agreement and approval. But this was all information his apprentice should know by now. He continued to question his helper as he soaked the captive's chains in the Wolfsbane water and locked him up with the chains hanging from the iron ring attached to the top of his crate. The man hung limply, still unconscious with his arms stretched above his head. It was easier to remember he was part human when his eyes and mouth were closed. Right now he looked more like the tired, beaten down prisoner he was rather than a dangerous, mythological creature.

The Collector

As Philip closed the large wooden box sealing the werewolf inside, he looked at the boy again. "And what about a faun, should we happen to have one on board, what does its safe confinement require?"

Stephen rattled off the correct response. "Muzzle over the mouth to prevent it tricking you with its lies, and a blindfold as well over the eyes so it cannot see its captors. And chains, of course, like all the others."

Fauns were certainly clever creatures, and their sharp wit and crafty tongues could spin a web of deception to which even the most experienced Collector could fall prey.

"How about a vampire?" Philip wasn't done yet.

"Locked in a wooden coffin, and pierced through the heart with a wooden stake." Stephen sent a nervous glance at the coffin propped up down the aisle. He didn't seem fully comfortable with his apprenticeship just yet. Philip understood, as it took time to adjust to the extraordinary, especially when it was extraordinarily dangerous.

"A witch?" He continued to regale the boy with questions about various creatures as they climbed the ladder and entered the primary hold full of their cover goods to sell upon return to England.

The boy answered, recounting just how they were holding their witch below for transport, and smiled when Philip gave him a nod of encouragement at all of his correct responses. Stephen was full of knowledge without a doubt, but forgetfulness would get you killed in this line of work, as certain as the snow that fell on a cold winter's night in the mountains. Something had to be done to help the lad not only retain the useful information but utilize it as well. In a job where your primary concern was escaping with your life, information had to be implemented or it died with its owner.

They clambered up the second ladder onto the deck. The morning light stabbed a welcome pain in Philip's eyes after the dark, grim holds beneath. A grey haze coated the sky, but some light shone through. Winter, mixed with the smoke coming from nearly every chimney in the city, created a smog and soot filled painting overhead. The ugliness overhead was still better than what lay below his feet though. He had been at this job of collecting creatures causing harm for nearly twenty-five years now, but he harbored no real affection for it. It was just something that needed doing and he was trained to do it.

"Oy, Philip," a voice called out from the captain's deck.

Turning his gaze from the sky, he saw his partner striding towards him down the steps to the deck where Philip stood. The newcomer was sturdily built in comparison to Philip's deceptively lean frame, with a layer of skin and fat over the thick muscles hidden below. Anyone or anything that thought James soft, however, would be in for a surprise if they decided to attack him. The man was strong, and had some nasty weapons at his belt to go with the arsenal of tricks he kept up his proverbial sleeve as well.

"We should make sail on the evening tide. I fancy the winds will be just right by then."

James functioned as the captain when they were on the ship. His previous experience of working in shipping yards and as a sailor prior to joining the Guild gave him the knowledge of how to steer their course correctly. Whereas Philip tended to take the lead when they left the sea and set foot on solid ground.

He nodded to his partner and friend of ten years. "We'll finish up this morning. I meet with Mr. Astori not long from now to see if he has any final instructions for us before we sail back to England and make a deposit in St Thomas."

Philip suppressed a shudder at the thought of the location to which they were transporting their cargo. It masqueraded as an insane asylum located on a small, remote port on the southeast corner of the English coast, but only those who belonged to the Guild knew what it truly was; a prison for the kind of things most people only saw in their nightmares.

Call them mythological creatures, monsters, legends, half-human or simply magical, it mattered not, they were a menace to society. Well, most anyway. He knew this because every Guild member was trained in the history and code of the Guild when they joined. Creatures who stayed quiet and didn't draw attention to themselves lived out their lives in relative peace, but if those same creatures succumbed to their baser natures and began terrorizing the regions in which they lived, then it fell to the worthy men and women of the Guild of Collectors to go deal with the situation by removing the threat and covering it up, if possible.

The Collector

He shook off his musings. "I'm headed there right now. Shouldn't be too long I don't think, unless Mr. Astori gives us one last assignment before we leave."

James sucked on his teeth and spat a glob of phlegm over the rail into the filthy port water lapping at the hull of the ship. "Say hello to your old friend for me," he said, his expression sour as he turned back to whatever task had been occupying him on the captain's deck before Philip and Stephen had exited the cargo hold.

"I will," Philip fixed a cool stare on his partner, "Martin Astori is my friend, James, and a senior member of the Collector's Guild. I have known him for years. Is there a problem?"

James paused and then spat again. "Nope, no problem." For a moment he appraised Philip, mouth pinched as if not sure whether or not to speak his mind. "It's just that there's something strange about that man. I can't put my finger on it, but mark my words, I can sense it."

He showed his yellowed teeth in an amiable grin and changed his tone. "Look, he'll probably send us on another bloody mission. Just watch." And with that James was back to his usual lighthearted self and began describing a serving girl at one of the bars downtown who had the roundest hips imaginable.

Apparently, he had gone there for a drink once and recommended Philip visit and procure her services. James told Philip that since he was going into town on business anyways, he might as well have some fun while he was at it.

Philip snorted and waved his partner's suggestions away. He had a far more respectable woman on his mind these days. But she lived on the outskirts of the city and he had already said his goodbyes to her for the coming voyage. He wasn't going to risk her safety by visiting her again so soon. Collectors tended to curry danger wherever they went, and he wanted to limit that element with her as much as possible. She was his secret and he meant to keep it that way.

He hadn't even told James about Alayna. The less people knew of her, the safer she would remain, and keeping her safe had become his goal. He sometimes wondered if that meant he loved her, but he wasn't fully ready to admit that to himself. As a sign, whenever they wished to see one another, they would send a small bouquet of pale blue Morning

Glories. The bouquet came alone, without a note, but the message was clear. Philip believed James had guessed that a girl had caught his eye, but his partner never asked. He respected Philip's privacy.

Philip left his thoughts of Alayna and went back to pondering his partner's odd hesitation at the mention of Mr. Astori. In the end he shrugged it off and prepared to leave the ship. James was a Guild member through and through, but he had chosen to enter the Guild at a later stage of life, as opposed to being practically born into it the way Philip had been. At times James found it hard to dedicate his every waking moment to the job. Philip guessed he was probably ready to go home to England to see his wife and daughter. Philip, on the other hand, had never known anything but the Guild life, and had no wife or children awaiting his return, so the length or duration of a mission did not matter. In fact, the closest thing he had to a wife was here in America, so he was more than happy to knock his boots around these streets for as long as the Guild officials deemed necessary.

He turned towards the gangplank connecting the ship to the wharf and left his partner and apprentice behind him. It was time to go. He had a meeting with Mr. Astori, and when one was meeting with a higher-ranking member of the Guild, it did not pay to be tardy.

Chapter Two

Philip stepped from the boarding plank onto the cobblestone quay and walked to the small, box-wagon, hitched next to the ship. This wagon was always the last item hoisted into the hold, since it was kept free until right before the ship set sail for last minute uses such as this. The red paint, once bright, but now faded and chipped from years of wear, boasted similarly faded gold lettering that read, "The Wheaton Brothers, Two Man Traveling Show."

The wagon gave the appearance of a two-man attempt at a carnival that had fallen upon hard times. He and James took it on Collection missions. The interior concealed all variety of useful tools for taking down their quarries. Nets soaked in Wolfsbane or garlic, back-up silver daggers and many more items that were crucial to the safety and success of their work for the Guild. Of course, they weren't brothers, it was just a cover, but it was the perfect way to transport their captives back to the ship and away from whatever location from which they had been collected.

Philip and James's line of work for the Guild involved what the rest of society deemed supernatural or extraordinary, and even those were the more generous terms that would be used should their work be discovered by the general public. Guild workers often used means such as this to transport their prey. After all, the best place to conceal the absurd and usually dangerous, was right in the middle of what society had already deemed bizarre. Most people saw the two-man carnival fallen on hard times, and overlooked any other strangeness attached to their actions, attributing it to the fact that in their minds, anyone who chose a life of wandering, performing, and poverty from the back of a tiny wagon was bound to be odd.

He stepped lightly up onto the seat and shook the reins to set the horses on their path into town. The streets were crowded, but people on foot made way for the wagon, since nobody wished to be trampled by the horses. As they rolled over the various unpaved alleys, the splatter of mud from the wheels and the creaking of the wagon's timbers mixed with the sounds of the city. Men looking for work by the wharf cried their talents, and the chatter of a hundred different conversations followed Philip as he rode along. Background noise, the symphony of life in New York City, and if Philip were completely honest with himself, he enjoyed it. The hustle and bustle of the city might wear a man down at times, it was true, but on a different day it could enliven him and set his blood pumping. It was a city full of vitality and energy.

When Philip reached the small square south of the docks, where he was supposed to meet Mr. Astori, he found it oddly quieter than the rest of the city. Pulling on the reins, he stopped the wagon at a place where he could hitch the horses. He found it cumbersome to navigate the creaky, old wagon through the city, but it was better than having to walk the entire way on only a few hours of sleep.

Philip leapt down from the seat and attended to his business of hitching the animals, then leaned against a small fence surrounding the statue in the middle of the square. Several minutes later he saw the familiar, limping figure of Mr. Astori heading in his direction from a side street.

Mr. Astori was dressed in his usual fashion, a black bowler on his head, a dress coat and pants over his boots. The entire outfit spoke of a gentleman just barely keeping his head above water. The shabby clothing served as a cover, of course, as the Guild richly supplied all financial needs of their members, but it was a necessary ruse to blend into the city. A man striving to better himself, one who'd just barely managed to do so after a lifetime of hard work, was the story of thousands here in the city. Mr. Astori blended in nicely.

As he approached, Mr. Astori smiled beneath the grey mustache that ran from the top of his lip down the sides of his mouth and hung just slightly below his chin. A thin smile, not overly welcoming, but that was

The Collector

his way. Mr. Astori might be a cold man, but his affections always seemed warmer for Philip than anyone else, even if that didn't amount to much. Ice was still ice, even when thawed slightly. Nevertheless, Philip's respect ran deeply for the man, even without a real bond of emotional unity between them.

"Good day, Sir," Philip inclined his head. "I was surprised to hear that you wanted to meet with me again before I leave since we spoke in depth not much more than a week ago."

Mr. Astori nodded his head in greeting as well. "Yes, I have some last minute business to which you must attend. It was necessary to speak to you in person." He shifted his weight to relieve the pressure on his legs and leaned more heavily on the cane clasped between his hands as its point pressed firmly against the cobblestones in front of him.

Philip understood. Life came at you from all different ways at once, and sometimes you just had to roll whichever way the seas of life tilted your deck. Squinting his eyes, he stared at Mr. Astori, the sun behind him making it difficult to see without doing so. He looked different than the last time they had met.

"May I say, you are looking particularly well, Sir," Philip phrased his compliment carefully; some people didn't appreciate them. "As if you have shrugged off a few years in the last week or so."

The senior Guild member cocked his head as if pondering something serious, and then cracked a rare, wrinkled smile, like sunlight glancing off a frozen pond. "Yes, my serving man Renold, has insisted that I begin taking long walks in the morning and eve to maintain my health."

"Well, it appears to be working," Philip raised his voice in order to be heard as the muffled din of the city surrounded them, carts rolling, people shouting and the occasional bark of a dog. He'd never heard that walking could cause this much of a shift in appearance over such a short time frame as one week, but after all, he had seen much stranger things in his line of work. After exchanging a few more pleasantries, they got down to the business at hand. Mr. Astori seemed preoccupied with his thoughts, only half answering some polite inquiries into the course of his previous week, so Philip reasoned his companion wished to complete their meeting.

Mr. Astori had a habit of keeping their encounters brief but at times he would linger just a bit and speak with Philip about things apart from work. The past and Philip's parents often served as the focus of those conversations, as Mr. Astori had been close with them in the years before their death. Philip enjoyed those times as much as any person did when hearing of one's parents from a friend's perspective. Yet he had moved far from a child who needed to hear the tales of his parent's accomplishments and deeds. He rather appreciated more the fact that a senior member of the Guild, and a role model to Philip, would care to build even a semblance of a relationship. But not today, this day Mr. Astori did not appear at all eager to be distracted with idle conversation.

"Perhaps we should proceed," Philip suggested. Mr. Astori inclined his head in agreement and immediately snapped into senior Guild member persona, leaving behind even his wintry smiles from earlier with only a mask of seriousness in its wake.

The old man cleared his throat. "It has come to the Guild's attention that there appears to be one more Collection that needs to take place before your departure for England." He paused to appraise Philip's face. "I trust there is no issue with that?" His eyes bored into Philip's, as if daring him to admit a problem with his orders.

"No, Sir, no problem at all," Philip responded, straightening his back subconsciously. "My partner and I are always ready for a mission, however impromptu it may be."

The Guild member nodded as if that was the most normal response. When a senior Guild member said hop, you hopped. You didn't ask why.

"Good, that's very good," Mr. Astori said, "but you will leave directly from here. It will be a solo collection. There is no need to return to the ship for your partner." The elderly man finished his sentence curtly and cast a fleeting glance at the street and the seeming chaos of the city at mid-morning, which surrounded them.

Philip nodded his head, processing the information. "I see." But then he decided to bring up a difficult issue. "I must inform you, Sir, that on our latest mission last night, my partner and I somehow became separated." Philip always disliked having to report failure, but in this case he felt obliged to do so.

The Collector

Thinking back to the previous night's encounter with the gypsy-lad, he continued. "The subject of my pursuit, some sort of half-breed, escaped. I couldn't catch him alone. I feel I must advise that I not go alone on this mission in light of this recent failure." Philip's lips pressed together in distaste as he closed his argument as respectfully as possible. Always a tricky situation, disagreeing with a higher-ranking member of the Guild.

Mr. Astori, responded with an impatient expression yet with uncharacteristic leniency in regards to Philip's admission. With a shake of his head, he disregarded the information. "No matter. What is done is done. The quarry from last night is lost, and you will still go on this last mission today alone. It is a matter of urgency, and we cannot wait for you to return to the ship and rouse your partner from a drunken slumber."

James was often, though not unfairly, viewed upon with disdain by many of the senior Guild members, and by Mr. Astori especially. Philip's partner enjoyed a drink more often than not, and once or twice had been unable to perform his duties when a mission came up due to inebriation. It had been years since that happened, but his reputation as an unreliable member had remained.

The response of Philip's overseer seemed strange in more ways than one. Mr. Astori was not a man known for mercy, even with Philip, and Philip's parents had worked closely with him prior to their deaths. So for his superior to disregard a failure such as last night without so much as a blink of an eye was uncharacteristic. And yet, at the same time, for him to advise going against Guild policy to take on a Collection mission alone was also not in his nature. Mr. Astori usually made his decisions based primarily upon the Guild rulebook and guidelines. The guidelines were clear; Collections were to be attempted in pairs to give the highest probability to avoid fatalities and ensure success. Seldom were solo missions allowed.

"Yes, Sir." Philip could only acquiesce. When a senior member gave an order, you followed it. The tension abated slightly with Philip's verbal retreat, but Mr. Astori still seemed vexed during the rest of his conversation, as if Philip's questioning his direction had left a bad taste in his mouth.

The senior member continued. "You will go alone," he emphasized again, "and you will go now, to the edge of the city limits." The old man's back remained stiff as a board as his gnarled hands grasped his cane and he gave his orders.

Once again, Philip couldn't help but be struck by the renewed youth in his face and stance. The man still had an elderly appearance, to be certain, but now he seemed to be not much over fifty years of age where as a week ago, a person would have been hard pressed to estimate him a day under sixty-five.

Mr. Astori pointed his cane. "There is an abandoned house on the south end of the city. Here is the address." He slipped Philip a piece of paper. "There you will collect any and all creatures that violate our protection code. Are we clear?" He ended with a pointed look at Philip as if daring him to speak out again.

"One question, Sir," Philip asked, "What do you mean by 'any and all'? I do not enjoy undertaking a mission without full disclosure of information, a fact you well know." He suppressed a feeling of frustration, as there were pieces of information that seemed to be lacking in this assignment.

Mr. Astori showed his teeth in an attempt to appear friendly but Philip knew that this was indeed only a hollow gesture. "A Vampire. Adult. Maybe a young one as well. That's all we know," he spoke his clipped sentences with a sour twist of his mouth. He looked the part of a querulous old gentleman indeed by this point.

"A young one?" Philip exclaimed in disbelief. He had only heard of that happening once in all of the Guild's history. Young vampires were a rarity for a number of reasons. "That should be entertaining," he finished bitterly. It was hard enough always capturing and keeping these things, *people*, he reminded himself yet again, without having to broaden his hunt to children. He didn't know how he would retain his humanity if he were forced to capture children, however monstrous they might be. Some things simply were not easy to stomach.

Mr. Astori caught his reluctance from the tone of his voice. "Is there a problem?" the old man asked in vexation, and not without an edge to his voice hinting at danger if there was an issue.

The Collector

Philip ignored the warning signs and answered, "Maybe. Maybe I am tired of always shooting, stabbing and bagging first, and talking second." Even as the words came out of his mouth, he knew they were idealistic. It never worked, to talk, but a part of him couldn't help but wish.

"And what would you prefer?" Mr. Astori asked. "You go out and you collect the mischievous, the dangerous, the overall menaces to society and you keep the world safe!" His attempt at encouragement fell short as Philip heard a hint of something bitter in the old man's voice as well. It was as if he couldn't even swallow what he was trying to force Philip to drink himself.

"Aren't they part of the world too?" Philip questioned, his heart heavy.

"What do you want me to say, boy?" Mr. Astori retorted gruffly. "Yes? That the world is one big mad house and humans and creatures alike deserve an equal share of it?" The old man paused and anger welled up on his face. "You and I of all the Guild members should understand that!" His frustration ebbed, replaced by only bitterness. "But Guild code says they aren't, and they don't. So we do our job and we keep the humans safe."

He imbued the word humans with as much disgust as one could, as if the idea of a race of people that, in large part, lived in the dark regarding the reality of the world around them was something of extreme distaste and disdain. It was true, most humans didn't even realize the Guild was protecting them, but that didn't mean that they didn't deserve protection. Philip could almost hear the confusion of his own inner monologue. Philip's mind was that of a man torn. On the one hand, many of these creatures posed a danger to anybody around them and had to be destroyed, but so many of his quarries had simply been scared half-breeds, a remnant or memory of the Great Transformation and all that it had entailed.

Philip continued, "Do you mean what I think you do when you spoke of us 'of all people'?" His question to Mr. Astori set the man to rubbing where his coat covered his wrist, as if there was something there that soothed his agitation.

"No, I meant nothing by that comment," the old man responded as if he was annoyed that he had mentioned it.

Philip didn't give up, but pressed a supposition he had entertained for years. Taking a gamble, he spoke out. "You have magic don't you?"

The old man's head whipped up in alarm, whether at a true statement or at an accusation that could have severe complications attached to it, Philip wasn't sure. Yet, Philip thought he knew the truth of it though, without even needing an answer. He was good at measuring men by their eyes and Mr. Astori's held the caution of a man who had revealed too much in a moment of lost composure.

Philip continued, "It happened during the Great Transformation, didn't it? It's how my parents saved my life when I was just a boy. You counseled them which action to take and what blood to use when I came down with the Shakefever. I would have died if you hadn't used your abilities, wouldn't I?" He paused, and then ended with a sense of gratitude, "I suppose I should be thanking you."

The senior Guild member's face had turned cold as stone. "There are some things, Philip, best left untouched, some things we can have no way of knowing. Wild guesses can create more trouble than good." It was not a pleased expression on Mr. Astori's face at Philip's thanks, nor was it an admission of whether the statement was true, yet Philip was convinced of it. This explained a lot. The senior member was known for his privacy and for keeping people at an arm's length, something necessary when housing a secret such as this.

Mr. Astori wasn't quite finished with his warning. "Some secrets are too dangerous to ferret out and should be best left alone."

Philip responded just as obliquely, "And some secrets are too potent to remain hidden from the people who know us well."

The senior member gave him a frosty stare and then nodded in what appeared to be a dismissal of the topic. He pivoted and walked a few steps before turning back to end the meeting once and for all. "Go to the address on the piece of paper. Do your job."

His lips twisted into a slight sneer, "I suppose you can handle two potential targets, yes? After all, two aren't that many. It isn't like it's the Great Transformation all over again," then he muttered under his breath, "Although that might not be half bad."

The Collector

Philip wasn't sure that he'd heard that last comment correctly and he found it odd, since the Great Transformation had been one of the darkest times in the world's history.

It had been an event unexplainable in origin, with effects that reached around the globe. In fact, the world still had not fully recovered from the destruction that had taken place after nearly forty years. There were whole towns and villages uninhabited and left to the wild now throughout America, Europe and the rest of the world.

The Great Transformation was a period of time when a land's myths and legends, fairy tales, and nightmares, had come to life.

Philip remembered the stories he had heard as a boy, as he watched his old acquaintance walk away. It was strange; Mr. Astori had seemed to be leaning fairly heavily on his cane at his approach to their meeting, but as he left there seemed to be an extra spring in his step, almost unbeknownst to the old man himself, and his usage of the cane was much less. Philip shook his head and shrugged off the oddity. In his line of work, if you spent all your time attempting to puzzle out the reason behind every strange occurrence, you would waste your life away.

His mind shifted back to the Great Transformation and all that it had been. Monsters rarely replicated as quickly, or as often, as their gruesome myths inclined hearers to believe. Many of the non-human or half-human beings Philip and the other Collectors were forced to pursue were dangerous, but they generally produced their trouble on a small scale and incidents were usually contained faster than anybody would imagine. The arm of the Collectors' Guild reached far and wide. Breakouts or epidemics of any of these creatures were not common. It had been that way for almost all of recorded history, the same trends, and patterns directing destiny for humans and supernatural beings alike. Not so during the Great Transformation.

Philip leaped agilely onto the wagon that was big enough for only one, maybe two captives at a time, and set off towards the outskirts of town in search of the address he had received from Mr. Astori. He couldn't help but wonder what it would have been like to be alive during the wild time in history. Things had changed almost overnight during the Great Transformation. All of a sudden, 40 years ago, a rash of outbreaks overtook the world.

Fairies in the British Isles began swarming the forests, playing their tricks on travelers. Witches in New England and magicians in countries like Egypt and Italy, had begun recruiting more heavily than normal. Trolls had woken from their snowy slumber in the Nordic countries, appearing en masse. People went to bed human and woke up as something much different. It was like a man's genetics were no longer set in stone. Even creatures that had to be turned or transformed from human state to creature, such as werewolves and vampires, suspended their normal processes. There had been reports of people waking up in the middle of the night with a hunger for blood and no reported bites or attacks to turn them into these monsters. It was as if the earth itself had decided to give birth to all of the native legends of all the separate lands simultaneously.

The records of history ran through Philip's mind like a theatre performance, as he weaved his way slowly towards his soon to be captive's location. All of his musings of the Great Transformation refreshed his memory as to where he was going and for what purpose. He was glad it was morning; morning was a good time to hunt vampires.

As he went, he remembered his parents telling him stories of what it had been like back then. They had told him of entire towns drowned in bloodshed as humans and supernatural beings alike butchered each other, in fear or in a simple response to a new nature imbued upon them. The Guild of Collectors had their work cut out for them in those times. It had taken years to put the world back together, and even after countless deaths and sacrifices on the part of the Guild and their Collectors, it just didn't quite seem like civilization had made a full recovery.

The leaders of the nations had met, counseled by the Guild, and had covered up what they could of the unbelievable nature of the preceding events. Many murders had been attributed to serial killers and normal criminal riffraff. They had called it a "plague of widespread insanity," and most city folk, who were inclined to dismiss superstition and magic, believed them. However, many in the country sides, where the transformations, deaths, and attacks had been the worst, knew better. They had seen too much for their brains to be washed by the governmental voodoo of world leaders. It was the way of life. Always it seemed, a large portion of the masses swallowed the reality given to

The Collector

them by society and by those in charge, while only a small, fringe element realized the truth.

Philip quit his musings and focused on the task ahead. His thoughts on society weren't really that important at the moment. More vital to him was a plan of how to survive the coming Collection. He placed his mind on the strategies he would use to gain success and rode onward focused, guiding the wagon toward the outskirts of the city and the duty that he had accepted the day he became a Collector.

Chapter Three

Philip's attention sharpened to a dagger's point as he entered what looked to be the neighborhood of his prey, judging by the instructions he had been given. He kept the wagon moving slowly as he looked every way at once. Vampires were among the most dangerous of quarries, and it paid to keep as vigilant a watch as possible. Philip shuddered to imagine what Romania must have been like during The Great Transformation. The Collectors' Guild had lost roughly one quarter of all of its Collectors trying to suppress the sudden flood of vampires swarming through Eastern Europe and terrorizing the night.

He felt an uncommon uncertainty about this mission. He was accustomed to having his partner with him to watch his back, and he rarely had been asked to take on one vampire, let alone the possibility of two, all by himself. Why had Mr. Astori sent him here alone? It was an unsettling question.

This far toward the outskirts of the city the buildings had changed. Well-formed homes and businesses made of lumber, and stone gave way to ramshackle huts and broken-down houses. Boards were nailed over windows where the glass had broken. Doors were ripped from their hinges, whether by storms or by something more sinister Philip didn't know, and had been left where they lay on the ground. The lack of doors on many houses gave the appearance of dirty monsters with gaping maws ready to swallow the unwelcome visitor.

Philip rarely let his imagination get away from him like this and he reined in his oddly colorful thoughts and focused on the task at hand—finding the address. There. The house for which he was searching

The Collector

loomed up from behind a cluster of buildings on his left. It looked like what must have been an attempt at building a mansion many years ago by some up-and-coming member of society, but whether for a lack of finances or some other unknown reason it had remained unfinished.

The top floors were open wide to the elements, and the bottom floor appeared the only one livable. But nothing was really livable in this dingy, corner of the city. It was even worse than the apartment into which he had followed his unbelievably quick, supernatural target last night. This house looked like all the rest in the neighborhood- brown and black from dirt and fires, and full of what almost certainly would be a host of unpleasant insects.

He stopped the wagon and dismounted the seat. His stomach had the nervous, fluttery feeling it always did before a Collection. You never knew what might happen when fists started flying and blood began flowing; there was always a risk involved. Yet, his nerves weren't a bad thing because they told Philip that he was still human and not desensitized to the potential of taking a life or of losing his own.

It was a common occurrence within the Guild. Collectors spent years corralling their victims, many deserving of course, but it added up. After so much time allotted to battle after battle to keep people safe, it was common for many Collectors to lose the empathetic bond between beings that signified they were still capable of feelings. It was as if somebody stuck their emotions on ice and numbed them to the core. James, Philip's partner, dealt with it as best he could by using humor or the occasional strong drink; something to which Mr. Astori had alluded. Philip on the other hand took a different approach. Instead of shunting away the pain and nerves, he welcomed them, embracing the flow of unease and caution, and even reticence to fight, as a signpost saying he was still a man, a person just like everyone else on the planet, regardless of how strong he was, or what he did as an occupation.

Philip opened the wagon's door and grabbed what supplies he might need as quickly as he could. It was late morning, which meant that the vampire, or possibly vampires, depending on the uncertain information provided by Mr. Astori, would be inside that house. Sunlight was their major weakness, and that meant their freedom to roam and feed took place during the darkness, under cover of clouds and the filmy light of the moon. Philip had an advantage in that if it were necessary in the upcoming confrontation, he would be able to retreat back out into the safety of the nearly noonday sun.

He grabbed a few normal wooden stakes, tucking two into his belt and one into each of his boots. Next, he doused his hands, face, and hair with water from the Hudson River. Vampires experienced difficulties with running water, although no one had reasoned out the cause. His jar full of river water wasn't running any more, but it still retained some of the properties that warded vampires away. It wasn't much help, but every little bit counted. When you got down to it though, a stake through the heart was really the only effective and completely proven method of vampire catching and killing.

Lastly, he chewed and swallowed two whole cloves of garlic to prevent sucking. If the worst happened and he wasn't able to capture or at least eliminate them, then he sure as stone didn't want to become a meal. Ingesting that much garlic right before the fight would ensure that he was as foul tasting to the dirty bloodsuckers as possible. They were once *humans*, he reminded himself. It was his latest attempt to remind himself to view them not just as an evil that needed to be eradicated. They were evil now, but they had once been part of humanity, and were now in need of being put out of their misery. He didn't know how vampires had originated, all he knew was that every documented case in the Guild's archives showed that they had once been humans, either turned by a bloodsucker, or indescribably changed into one during the Great Transformation.

The Great Transformation was an anomaly, nothing like it had ever happened before, and nothing since. Ninety-nine out of one hundred times the vampires he Collected had become one at the hands of another vampire. That meant that most of them were victims of poor choices. It was important to remember that when trying to preserve your own humanity. Although all the attempts in the world couldn't make it easier to forget that while this was true, many had embraced their lifestyle of bloodletting.

Preparations done, Philip grabbed one more stake for good measure, and walked swiftly and silently up to the front of the rundown house. The door creaked as he cautiously pushed it open with his left hand, right

The Collector

hand poised and ready with the stake to fight should the need arise. Philip stepped into the gloom and wished he had James to watch his back. Vampires tended to be one of the nastier creatures the Guild was required to collect, and it wouldn't hurt to have another set of eyes, especially if there really were two of the leeches. Once they were *men*, the thought floated across his mind absently.

He glanced around the interior of the room, taking in the scenery in a heartbeat, a talent he had picked up from years of being forced to survey a scenario in a moment's time. The room was drab and smelled musty, as if mold and cobwebs had formed atop generations of filth. A plain chair with no cushion was in the center of the room on a wooden floor. Lamps were non-existent; vampires could see well in the dark, and preferred the absence of light. Walls, of some type of dark wood, were spotted and pitted with age, and also with what looked like old blood. So he was in the right place. Vampire nests always tended to be free of clutter yet overwhelmingly covered with the remnants of their victim's blood.

Nothing moved. The house seemed as quiet and still as the sea on a storm-less summer morning. This did not bode well. It implied that they were ready for him and had concealed themselves, possibly having heard his wagon arrive. He imagined that visitors to this abandoned section of town weren't the norm, and his arrival must have stuck out like a sore thumb. There was nothing for him to do but to proceed. A mission was a mission, and he had been in sketchier situations than this and had survived to tell the tale.

Through a doorway to his left, he entered another empty room. His Collector's senses were tense, and he could feel that an attack was imminent. Sure enough, as he took another step into the middle of the room, the closet door in front of him shattered into pieces as the vampire burst from its hiding place. It tackled him to the ground before he could react but the thing's momentum sent them rolling backward together, and Philip, trained by his many confrontations such as this, harnessed their momentum by jamming his feet up under the vampire and by flinging it over his head as he did a backwards summersault. The beast crashed into the wall near the ceiling and then flopped to the floor.

Philip stood unsteadily as he tried to shake the fog from his brain that had occurred after the first impact of the vampire's attack. The creature stood up warily, as well, looking none the worse for wear. Vampires were resilient. They didn't heal quickly the way stories said, yet injuries definitely did not slow them down the way they did a human, so it amounted to much the same thing.

They eyed each other a moment, appraising each other, and then Philip felt a sharp pain in his hamstring. He looked behind him to see the smallest vampire he had ever laid eyes upon biting him. Not for the first time Philip was thankful that a simple bite couldn't turn one into a vampire. If that were the case, he would have become one long ago. It was just about impossible for one to tangle with a vampire and not receive at least one bite. No, vampires could only turn a willing victim.

Details were fuzzy, but from what the Guild knew of all the changings, excluding the Great Transformation, a person had to determine in his heart to accept the bite and desire to become a vampire for the change to take place. Maybe it was some chemistry between the brain and the body that Philip along with everyone else didn't understand, or possibly it was simply a mystery of the supernatural kind, one that would remain unknown. However, one thing was certain within the Guild, only someone who chose to be a vampire would actually become one. It lent a certain disdain to the way Collectors viewed them. Unlike a werewolf who's bite could turn even an unwilling victim on a full moon and during the right physical conditions, nearly every vampire had chosen or been tricked into a life of malice and death.

The small vampire clenched tightly to Philip. It had its mouth and teeth latched onto him and he spun quickly to try and disengage it. The little beast wouldn't let go. He finally managed to grab a handful of its hair to wrench it off of him. He threw the vampire toward the wall near its elder compatriot and it hit its head and slumped, stunned against the wooden support. The adult vampire sneered at the young one and bared its fangs at Philip.

"You were a fool to come alone," the thing whispered in an oddly seductive voice, like a siren calling to its prey. "I am too fast, too strong, and far too hungry for you to escape with your life."

The Collector

Philip felt a shudder run through him as the voice caressed his mind. Vampires had a few weapons in their arsenal, not the least of which was their silken vocal chords. Among the known capabilities of vampires, was their ability to impose their will upon another. It wasn't an exact science, and it sometimes didn't work. But the faint of heart, and weak of will, might find themselves doing things they never intended when facing the wrath of a vampire in the mood to toy with them.

Philip was strong mentally, coached and practiced in the arts of resisting will-bending. It was a requirement of Guild policy that each recruit undergo training in this capacity, therefore the vampire's suave voice provided only a slight tug on his mind and emotions.

Philip summoned up a chuckle and responded as he held his wooden stake ready. "That voice of yours is at odds with your appearance." The vampire was dressed in plain, dirty clothes resembling more of a country farm worker rather than the sultry, seductive tempter it hinted at being. "Your tricks won't work on me," he added in a more serious tone, as he tightened his muscles and prepared to spring.

"Well, in that case," the thing responded in a thick, coarse voice that must have been its natural form when abandoning its dangerous vocal tactic, "we may as well get on with it." It smirked at him evilly. "We both know that I'm faster and stronger than you. Let's not make this harder than it needs to be. Just put down the stake, and I'll finish you quickly and painlessly." The vampire's eyes hardened. "I may not even eat you, if you've swallowed even half as much garlic as it smells like you have."

It was true, the thing was quicker, but it didn't have all of the facts right. Philip felt the inward satisfaction of knowing that once again, his opponent had underestimated his strength, judging him only by the appearance of his slender frame. It was the courtesy of an infirm childhood—a gift from his parents, and from recent discovery, Mr. Astori, although the old man's reluctance to answer his question had left a small doubt. Nevertheless, the omission had been proof enough of the man's involvement. Philip's gift of strength beyond the normal human ability was a secret he kept close. Other than his parents' old friend, and Guild member Mr. Astori, only his partner James knew about it, and perhaps the victims of his Collecting he supposed, although they wouldn't have had an explanation for the reason.

Declining to respond to the vampire's taunt, Philip sprung forward swinging his stake toward the creature's heart. The vampire was quick, that was certain. It blocked his downward stroke with its arm, jarring the first stake loose from Philip's grip and sending it clattering to the ground on the far side of the room. The vampire looked surprised by the force with which Philip had swung his weapon, and he could see the seeds of fear growing in the vampires pitch-black eyes.

Without bothering to grab another stake, Philip defaulted to his preferred method of combat—hand to hand, fist to face, slug-it-out tactics. His deceptively small fists pummeled the vampire's body, weakening the creature with every blow. He forced it up against the wall, working it as a boxer worked a harried opponent on the ropes. The young one still lay, eyes glazed, against the wall.

The vampire hissed in frustration and blocked as best it could, overpowered by Philip's superior strength. Philip cocked his arm back quickly to deliver the final blow and it proved to be a poor choice. As he swung his fist mightily, the thing optimized on the delayed instant before the blow and utilized its speed to dart away from him. Philip's fist crushed through wood and he left a hole in the wall. Philip turned to the other side of the room, as he picked a few large splinters from his knuckles. His fists were callused and rough from brawling with many supernatural opponents, and felt less pain than they once had when he was younger.

The vampire looked at him with hatred and it was Philip's turn to experience a flicker of uncertainty and doubt, even fear as the thing advanced on him. It had weathered the initial onslaught and the surprise of Philip's first attack. Now it was time for it to work to its strengths-movement and agility. It stayed clear of his fists and delivered a series of slashing blows from the sharp fingernails it possessed. The nails couldn't quite be called claws, but they left gashes in Philip's arms and face from their passing. The vampire retreated a few yards back as it planned its next lunge. It smiled maliciously at Philip as it licked his blood from its fingertips.

The Collector

"Not too bad, considering it's saturated with garlic," the vampire commented, eyes narrowed. It had an unshaven face, sunken cheekbones, and a thin, wiry frame. The clothes it wore hung baggy on it, as if drinking blood didn't quite flesh a creature out the way normal food did.

Philip panted a moment and tried to regain his breath and energy after a string of lightning-quick assaults by the evil being. The vampire sensed its advantage and advanced once again. It rushed him, fangs protracted, and Philip only narrowly avoided what would probably have been a fatal bite to his throat, as he attempted to dodge and the fangs of the vampire sank deeply into his shoulder muscle. He grabbed it by the neck and ripped it off of him, casting it as hard as he could to the floor. Blood flowed copiously out of his shoulder, as he exploded downward in a flurry of fists only to smash the floor to pieces where the vampire had previously been.

It smirked yet again from across the room to where it had momentarily fled. "I told you, you're not fast enough," the vampire gloated.

"We'll see," Philip responded and took the fight to it. He pulled a stake from his belt and threw it like a knife piercing the vampire through the stomach. It grunted and stumbled backward as it clawed frantically at its belly to yank out the wood. The injury slowed the thing down somewhat, and Philip knew from experience that wood-inflicted injuries caused vampires no end of pain, but the vampire still continued its fast string of attacks. It was too much for Philip to handle. Philip wished in vain that one wound could have slowed the vampire down more than it appeared to have done.

And then the worst of it came, as Philip had known it would. It began employing the most dangerous of all of its abilities, and Philip was hard pressed to do anything but survive. Vampires were known to have speed, strength, and siren-like voices, but their most dangerous talent was an enhanced predatory instinct. Predators around the world in the animal kingdom could sense fear, and weakness, using that knowledge in an instinctual manner to figure out how to best attack their prey. Vampires, being predators of a different and far more immoral kind, utilized the same tactics. Vampires were known to be able to pinpoint a person's weak spots without being told, almost like a psychic ability developed as they changed away from being humans and into their current, blood-lusting state of being.

This particular vampire somehow locked in on the fact that Philip had some minor wounds, patched up from the encounter the night before. His clothing hid them, but the creature pinpointed them all the same. It began striking his wounds, which had only begun to heal, sapping his energy quicker than he would have thought possible. It struck the deep bite on Philip's shoulder, and even managed to discern a slight limp that he carried in his left leg due to an old injury to his knee. The vampire targeted the weak knee and struck it repeatedly, swerving in time and time again to strike the different weak points on Philip's body. It was a supernatural ability coupled with a faster than human creature. As a result Philip could feel his body deteriorating and his energy sapping more rapidly than normal. His muscles lost strength; his eyesight grew blurry from pain and fatigue. He pulled the last stake from his belt and chucked it as hard as he could, but the vampire dodged his throw easily this time, snickering as it slipped eel-like out from the path of the sharp wood.

The vampire delivered a final crushing blow to his bitten hamstring and then his weakened knee and Philip slumped to his knees in exhaustion. The vampire had worn him down. This was why Collectors were always advised to go in pairs. If James were here to work together with him, the vampire would be the one at a disadvantage, not Philip. Why had Astori sent him alone? The odds were never in one's favor in a one on one fight with a vampire.

The creature danced around to the front of him and grasped his hair hard, pulling his head back and forcing his back to arch painfully, as it stared malevolently into his eyes.

"I don't care that you taste bad, do you hear me?" the thing began. "You Collectors think you are invincible." The bloodletting being had hate in its eyes and delight on its evil face as it continued. "I'm going to eat you and enjoy how revoltingly pleasant it is to drink from a Collector who thinks that a little garlic is going to keep me from enjoying such a worthwhile meal."

The Collector

Philip wobbled slightly with fatigue and the vampire smiled as it saw how weak and tired he was. It appeared that even Philip's enhanced strength could not override the exhaustion caused by the hundreds of tiny injuries covering his body. It was a sobering thought as death stared him in the eyes.

"Tell me I am better than you," the vampire dropped its natural, hardened voice and whispered in a soft silky tone. "Tell me that you wish you were me."

It was employing its vocal abilities again and Philip was hard pressed to keep his lips clamped shut and avoid giving it the pleasure of this final indignation. It seemed that death had finally come for Philip after all these years, but he was not about to resign himself to the humiliation that would ensue from giving this creature the ugly pleasure of manipulating his mind. If Philip's mind had possessed heels, he would have described it as digging them in, and concentrating on the fight for his dignity that was the last battle remaining to him.

Then all of a sudden, when all hope was lost, the most confounding thing happened. The vampire's hair turned grey, and his nails shriveled. Wrinkles appeared en masse on his middle-aged face and sags of skin began to droop under his chin.

The vampire felt the changes, frantically shook Philip, and screamed, "What are you doing to me? How are you doing this!" The vampire was almost in hysteria now as its hair had turned completely white, and the muscles in its arms began to flesh out and droop as if they were becoming old and fatigued in the space of a few moments.

Philip had no idea why luck was favoring him this way but he decided to keep the thing talking to distract it. "Oh, I think you know what I'm doing," he said, feigning an understanding that he did not possess. He would have said anything to keep the vampire off its guard and in a state of shock.

The vampire's eyes widened in terror, "Did *he* send you? Tell him to take it away. I don't want this curse! It isn't fair!" the creature wailed.

Philip's hand crept to the stake hidden in his right boot as the vampire stared frantically into his eyes searching for an answer that wasn't there. The vampire seemed to have aged into an old man in the course of a few moments time, whatever youth had been there was now gone.

Philip got a good grip on his weapon and then exploded into action with the last reserves of his strength, plunging the stake with force into the vampire's unsuspecting heart. The creature collapsed and then shriveled in upon itself in a wild fashion. By the time the thing fully died, the body had shrunk to one-half of its normal size, and looked as if it had been buried for years and then dug up. This was something Philip had never encountered before. Something odd was at play. What could steal a being's power, its youth, and vitality? The answer eluded him, and he pulled his weapon from the body. The tip of his stake was burnt and black in an unusual manner. Fortune had certainly shined upon him today, his survival was proof of that, however, he couldn't help but feel uncomfortable with the fact that there were things going on here that Philip couldn't explain.

The little vampire was still in a daze. Philip walked over to it and nudged it carefully with the tip of his already used stake. The thing slowly awakened from its stunned stupor, and as it did Philip crouched down in front of it, pondering what to do. It was little enough that he was certain he could capture it, even in his weakened state, but if he could convince it to come quietly, it would be better for both of them.

The creature finally seemed to clear its head enough for Philip to recognize the focus in its eyes. It was truly awake now, and he was hoping it would stay compliant.

Philip gazed steadily into its eyes. He had a simple manner about him. People always told Philip that he had a trustworthy face and honest eyes. He hoped that the vampire would see that and listen to his offer.

"You don't have to die." Philip wasn't one to dance around a topic. "Just come with me, nice and quietly, and I promise I won't kill you." He hefted the stake in his hand and gave the creature the most dangerous look he possessed. "And you know I could if I wanted. I've already taken care of your comrade." He glanced meaningfully at the husk of a former vampire behind him.

He could tell the creature understood him by the light in its eyes, but it refused to answer. Anger was present in its face, and more than a little bit of fear.

The Collector

He felt pity. It wasn't old enough to have truly embraced the ways of its newfound nature. It couldn't be more than seven or eight years of age, but that was assuming it had been recently turned. Vampires didn't age the way humans did, so he supposed it could have been changed even younger, and only now reached this stage in its appearance.

Still the vampire stared at him without answering and Philip was beginning to reach an end to his patience. He tried again, however.

"Was that your father?" he asked, delving deep within his empathetic reservoirs to draw upon as much compassion as he could. It was hard, but he managed to imagine what it was like to lose a vampire compatriot.

The thing shook its head. No. He supposed that made sense after all, seeing as vampires didn't breed the way humans did. It stood to reason that the dead one wasn't its father.

"Well then, was he the one who turned you?" The question was again met with a shake of the head. Philip couldn't see where this one-sided conversation was going. It was beyond his area of expertise; he was no interrogator. Not knowing what to say, he simply waited to see if the thing would eventually speak. He kept his hand ready with the sharp, wooden weapon.

Finally, the boy vampire relinquished his hold on silence and volunteered the beginning of a story. "He ain't turned me. Didn't no vampire turn me." It spoke with the accent of an unschooled, wilderness child, grammar, and vocabulary all a jumble of incorrectness and errors. His words however, chilled Philip to the bone. If no vampire had turned him, what did that mean? Was this the beginning of another Great Transformation? If that was the case, the world was in for a rough time, and the Guild council needed to know as soon as possible.

The thing continued as it saw that Philip offered a willing ear. Philip also supposed, rather ruefully, that it saw the stake in his grasp and had interpreted it as a non-negotiable request for its story. Philip had to concede that this was probably true. There was no way out of this situation for the little vampire but to talk. It was outsized, out-matched, and intimidated. That was good; he wanted the thing to be more than a little afraid of him. The more fearful it was, the less likely he would have to slay it.

"Yarrel," the little one nodded over to the dead vampire, "he found me 'bout a month back and he done let me stay here with him." The vampire actually looked like it was about to cry. Philip supposed that just because a vampire became a vampire didn't mean it automatically left behind all of its human emotions. Perhaps it never did.

Philip quirked his mouth sympathetically and asked, "So if he didn't turn you, then who or what did?"

"A man did. Really, really old man. He said..." The thing paused and hiccupped back a sob. "Said he could fix me, seein' as I couldn't walk and such." It finished in explanation to Philips cocked head.

"You were sick?" he asked the little vampire.

"Crippled," it responded despondently. "He said he could make me better. I jus' wanted to run again. Didn' know I was gonna be this." And then he really did break down and wail as he motioned to the tiny vampiric teeth in his mouth. The boy cried tearless sobs for a few minutes as Philip waited as patiently as he could for the next part of the story.

One side effect of the change was the bloodlust; another was the lack of other liquids within the body. Therefore, a vampire never shed tears, since it was unable. He felt genuine sorrow for the boy. It was easier to think of it as being still human, knowing that it hadn't truly chosen this life. Someone had deceived it, completely, utterly and with a more twisted agenda than anyone of which he knew.

"You really ain't goin' to kill me, mister?" the boy asked, still afraid that his question would be met with a swift and fatal response. "Yarrel, he said that people don't let vampires live if they knows that they's vampires."

Philip nodded. "Yes. You'll live." He tried to make his voice sound as calming as possible. "I'm a Collector, you know what that means, right? I suspect Yarrel mentioned us. And well, we don't kill when we don't have to." However, Philip's attempt at a compassionate response only set the thing to screeching.

"You're a Collector!" it screamed in terror. "Him that did this to me was a Collector. Get away from me!" The little vampire shot to its feet in defiance born of fear and began trying to fight its way clear of Philip's hands restraining it. It lunged this way and that, all the while nipping at

The Collector

Philip's forearms and hands, which were the only parts of Philip's body within reach of its mouth.

Philip's confusion at the thing's sudden hysterics, coupled with his own general lack of expertise with children, left his attempts at comforting platitudes raining upon deaf ears. The thing shouted and screamed for him to leave it alone for about half a minute before all too quickly it too began to shrink and shrivel, and dry up from the outside in. The thing's hair grew white immediately and the same process as had occurred with the elder vampire happened with the younger one, only much quicker.

In what seemed like less than a few heartbeats the thing was dead on the floor where it had fallen, leaving Philip speechless in response to these recent turns of events. James, he was sure, would have had some witty remark about having two less vampires to deal with on their own and how the mystery was a good one. But Philip was too shocked by the boy's claims of being turned by a Collector to be able to summon up such a cheeky thought the way his partner could. This was serious. Philip could feel something dark and sinister afoot.

He stood over the young, fallen vampire. He hadn't even struck it, only restrained it. That alone was proof that although he had provided the finishing blow for the older one earlier, they both would have been dead eventually, regardless of a stake in the heart or not. What had triggered these events? He couldn't believe that they just happened to occur right when he showed up. That did not fit with logic or reason. Therefore, it was safe to say that something triggered the sapping of their life. What had his arrival forced them into? The only thing he could think of was that it forced them to fight, although how fighting could make a thing shrivel up and die he had no idea. Not to mention the fact that he had been fighting and nothing had happened to him. The whole occasion was full of unsettling information. Vampires that shriveled and died, and a Collector who, allegedly, had somehow found a way to transform boys into young denizens of the city; it was all too much to ponder right now.

Philip trudged back to his wagon in exhaustion and grabbed his matches and some oil. These bodies had to be disposed of. As unlikely as it seemed that someone would stumble across them here in this empty nest of a shantytown, he still had to follow Guild procedure.

Mathias G. B. Colwell

The Guild guidelines stated that in the event of a death on the job, the creature must be disposed of as quickly and with as little evidence of its existence as possible. The idea was to keep as much of society living in relative naiveté, and innocence, an unconcerned reality of peace and happiness. Whether the efforts of the Guild truly achieved that or not, Philip wasn't at all certain. What he did know was that enough of the world lived an existence of poverty and striving that he wasn't sure their reality was that much better. Although on the other hand, maybe preventing the widespread awareness of the creatures of the underworld that could snap them in two at the drop of a hat and drink their blood, was a kindness. Maybe the Guild prevented this knowledge of a darker, more sinister reality, keeping it from being the straw that broke the camel's back, as the old saying went.

He wasn't sure what he thought exactly. What he did know, was that he felt weary, bone weary, in a way that had nothing to do with the fight. He was growing tired of all the dying. Philip reminded himself often that what he did was important, that he protected people, but there were moments in his job, like this, where he found it hard to reconcile that idea with reality. That young vampire's behavior had brought to mind the personality of the young boy he had been, more than the cold-blooded killer Philip had always supposed vampires to be. Even though Philip didn't think that he was directly responsible for the boy's death, it was difficult not to chalk this death up to the Guild and its tactics, as the fighting seemed to have precipitated its condition. The boy's death felt unnecessary, and it was hardly the first time he had killed a creature in his line of work. You could only tell yourself so many times that a creature merited killing, especially if that truth was questionable like it felt today, before it began to sound hollow.

He left his thoughts in the wagon and returned with the implements necessary to burn the bodies. He poured oil on one withered shell of a body and then the next. Then he lit the match and set them both ablaze. He watched until all but a bit of crispy remnants of clothing and bone remained before he left the house for good, and reentered what was now the afternoon sun. Sometimes the sun felt like a purifying force on his body. He spent so much time hunting his quarries at night that at times sunlight felt almost like a cleansing bath.

The Collector

He drank in the rays for a few precious moments and then lingered for even a few instants longer than he normally would have done. The morning had been full of a series of unforeseen events. It had begun with the startling revelation that Mr. Astori was hiding something akin to Philip's inhuman strength, showing that he did not adhere as closely to the Guild's doctrine as Philip had thought. And it had continued with a child vampire turned by what Philip could only describe as a Collector gone bad. It was more than he could process.

He mounted the seat of the wagon and shook the reins to start the horses moving. Whether he understood it all or not, it didn't change the fact that he had to get back to the ship. Philip could process on the journey home.

Death had almost come for him today. It was not the first time in his many years of Collecting that he had nearly come out second best in a confrontation with another being, but today had surely been close. That vampire today had been particularly adept at tuning in to its predatory intuition, more than most he had encountered. Certainly before, none had ever been able to pinpoint his weak knee. It was an old injury, and a limp he tried hard to conceal. The body part gave a twinge of pain, almost as if thinking of it produced that very result.

Philip shook the reins again absently, as if his subconscious wished to reach the ship sooner than his conscious mind realized. He set his course homeward, or at least to as much of a home as he had in this land, and tried to focus on the fact that he was still alive. That was something to celebrate. He told himself this over and over again as he did his best to shut off for a time the questions that did their best to gnaw incessantly at his mind. In the end he prevailed, and let his mind drift. If there was one thing he had learned in all of his years, it was that there were times to focus and times to unwind. This was a time to let go of everything and regain whatever measure of peace that he could. Philip leaned back against the wagon seat, relaxed his body as best he could and watched the road pass by.

Chapter Four

The trip back to the ship was lost in idle musings and the simple joy of the winter sun on Philip's face. It passed quickly and he reached the docks sooner than he had expected. Upon his arrival at the wharf in front of his ship, he could tell something was wrong. There was a stillness to the air and a quiet beyond that which should have been expected. He should have heard James shouting orders and curses at the crew, or for that matter, trading jokes with them as they prepared the ship to set sail. Something was amiss, and he aimed to find out what it was.

He checked the assortment of weapons concealed about his body to reassure himself. One stake remained hidden in his left boot, a silver dagger up his sleeve and another normal dagger at his waist. He fingered the knife at his waist absently as he strode across the gangplank and onto the ship. There was no doubt about it. The ship was in disarray. Boxes of goods lay strewn about the deck next to dead crewmembers that must have died while carrying them. It was unclear as to the cause of their deaths. Some harbored burn marks, others shallow wounds, but in general none looked to be the type of injuries that would prove fatal. It was yet another mystery to add to the day, another unanswered question hinting at foul play of the worst kind—magic. There were many creatures he pursued who killed by means of supernatural abilities, but the worst of those were the ones who murdered with magic.

Philip knelt by the first of the crew members to check, against hope, for a pulse and found none. It was the same with the next three. He glanced up high to the captain's deck but saw nothing and nobody. It was time to proceed to the lower levels of the ship, the cargo holds. Philip felt

The Collector

a great sense of trepidation as he imagined what the scene might be below. If the deck was this bad, he wasn't sure what to expect as he continued his investigation of the holds.

He climbed down the ladder and through the first, normal cargo hold without seeing a single person. He wasn't sure if that was a good sign or a bad one. The next hold of cargo, the ship's true purpose for travel back across the Atlantic to England, was another matter.

He stepped lightly and as quietly as possible from the ladder and surveyed his hold. It was thrashed. Boxes and crates were broken to pieces and sprayed about the floor like kindling. Cages with bars were open, their gates hanging loosely on their hinges. Not a single one of their captives remained, which boded ill for the future. This cargo hold had contained upwards of thirty different types of dangerous beings, the subjects of months of pursuit and capture up and down the Eastern seaboard. If they had all been let loose upon New York City at once, the results could be catastrophic.

A noise from the right side of the cargo hold caught his attention and he made his way over carefully to find out what it was. It was the weakest of weak breaths being inhaled and exhaled, as if each one was of great effort. When he saw James slumped against the wall of the ship, head dangling to one side as if the effort of holding up his head was too great for his neck, the worst was confirmed.

Philip rushed over to his partner. James had a hole in his chest clear through. It wasn't huge, but it was probably the size of a coin, enough to kill a man surely. The blood didn't flow from the hole like a normal wound; instead the edges of the injury were cauterized all the way through to his back. It was as if somebody had shot a fiery bullet clean through his partner's chest. He squatted down quickly, hoping to find a way to save his friend, but it was clear by looking at the wound that it had cut through parts of his vital organs. Philip was no surgeon, but he was pretty sure that the hole in James chest was located right where a lung was. It accounted for the horrible, wheezing breaths that his friend was attempting to take.

A hand gripped weakly at his leg as he knelt down and Philip glanced up from the wound to look his friend in the eyes. They were glazed with the fog of pain and death. Philip knew that these were his friend's last moments and he forced back his emotions in order to stay strong for James.

"Magician's fire, I think," he mumbled, nearly incoherently. He must have seen Philip studying the hole in his chest. It made sense. Magic could certainly do this. However, there were not many magicians capable of shooting fire this big since magicians tended to rely more on charlatan tricks and slight of the hand than real magic. Most magicians were usually half-breeds, not particularly strong, and they often used what magic they had to make money, not kill people. Fireballs were new to Philip since the most he had ever really seen before were sparks.

"We'll fix you up." Philip offered the empty, yet comforting, platitude to James, but the man squeezed his hand more tightly, as if using all of his remaining strength just to keep Philip focused on something more important. James was carefree and even reckless at times. This personality trait had lent him a rather cavalier attitude towards death. It appeared that actually facing that most dreaded of all enemies, one's own mortality, had done nothing to change his opinion of it.

His partner blinked blearily. "No. Forget about me," he barely managed to wheeze and then seemed to change subjects. "I told you he couldn't be trusted." The comment sent a cold shiver up Philip's spine. Who had he trusted that James had warned him not to? It was yet another puzzle of which he would have to riddle his way out.

James gasped his last breath and with it said, "Tell my family…" and then he was gone. He didn't finish the sentence but Philip was certain he would have said to tell his wife and kids that he loved them. He had always been a family man. It was the reason he had joined the Guild of Collectors in the first place. Once he had awakened to the truth that there were monsters of which to be wary and dangers in the night, he couldn't abide doing nothing when thinking of what might happen to his family if they stumbled across one of the creatures. It had been a matter of responsibility. He may not have enjoyed it, as it had often separated him from his family for months at a time, but he had accepted it and taken the charge bravely. Philip doubted he would ever have a truer friend or partner.

The Collector

He gently closed his dead partner's eyelids. There was something inhumane about leaving the dead with their eyes open. To do so would have felt like making James face the unknown of the great beyond without his eyes, as they were stuck staring lifelessly into the world he had just left behind forever. It was only a superstitious feeling, but Philip couldn't shake the truth that the dead were supposed to have their eyes shut, and living lived with theirs open. It was the way of it. There would be time for burials and tending to the dead later, however, Philip knew that most urgent at the moment was to notify the various Guild officials in the city of the attack and about the escaped supernatural creatures. One or two of those beasts free in New York would have been bad enough and he didn't want to think of what the whole lot of them would do.

Philip left James in the cargo hold for the moment, and felt a wrenching inside his gut as he did so. It wasn't supposed to be like this. Sometimes Collectors died in the line of duty, but not attacked while on their own vessels. This was supposed to be their safe haven. It was almost as if the last mission alone and the mission last night where he had become separated from James had been foreshadowing the death to come, an unwanted symbolic image of what life as a lone Collector would be like. Philip knew that the Guild would assign him another partner eventually, but right now all he had to address the situation at hand was himself.

The climb back to the deck was the longest of his life. How had this happened? It was the worst of a long line of mysteries that had complicated this day to no end. On deck, he walked back to the ship's two cabins, one for him, and one for James. It seemed impossible that anyone would have survived this attack, but he had not yet seen Stephen's body and he had to look. Philip opened the door to his cabin and walked inside. It was a small room by the standards of any home, but big for a ship of this size. A desk was nailed to the floor with a chair in front of it. There was a bunk big enough for only one person to sleep on at a time, and a lamp beside it. Philip's hopes swelled as he saw two feet poking out from under the desk. He bent down and sure enough, there was Stephen. His young face was streaked with tears and his hair was disheveled, as if he had spent the last few hours clutching his hands over his head and ears in an attempt to lock out the reality of the death and dying that had taken place onboard the ship.

Philip reached his hand out gently to the boy. "Stephen, it's alright. You can get up and come with me."

The boy opened his eyes and saw the familiar face in front of his. The absolute terror that had been written all over his features began to smooth as the realization that hope was not lost and his death wasn't around the corner. Then it was as if everything came crashing down again and he began to heave huge, gut-wrenching sobs. Philip hadn't known that there were that many tears in a person.

Philip was out of his element. Crying children were not his area of expertise and yet somehow this was the second time today that he had been forced to deal with one.

"It's safe now, Stephen, you're safe." He tried to calm the boy as he put a hand on his shoulder. "Whoever did this is gone now."

The boy gulped back a sob and nodded his head reluctantly. "I just hid, sir. I didn't do anything but run in here and hide." The shame in his voice was palpable and suddenly Philip knew what Stephen's fresh wave of sobs was all about. The boy was ashamed of not having fought against the attackers; as if a twelve year old kid would have been able to do anything other than get himself killed. The sentiment was an honorable one, Philip supposed, but he didn't have time to deal with hysterical remorse, however honorable it was.

"You did right, son." Philip attempted to console the boy and get him on his feet. "There was nothing you could have done. We don't pay you to fight just yet and that won't come for many years." He paused and tried to capture the boy's stare. "Besides, if you had fought you would certainly have died, and then I wouldn't have anybody left to help me. And you do want to help me, don't you?" The question he posed to Stephen coupled with the idea of having something important to accomplish seemed to perk the lad's spirits up somewhat. He wiped his nose with the back of his hand and did his best to stiffen his back.

"Of course I do, Master Philip. Whatever you need." He probably would have saluted to emphasize his newfound commitment to duty if Philip hadn't clapped him on the shoulder amiably as he gave him a fierce grin of approval.

The Collector

"Good. That's what I like to hear." Philip encouraged him. "What I need from you, Stephen, is to be my runner."

The boy waited for more information as Philip continued to explain. "I need you to carry a message to these locations," Philip said seriously, as he handed him a list of addresses of the four Guild members he knew of in the city. "Can you do that? I'll need you to be swift and sure. You just deliver one message and then move on to the next."

Stephen affirmed that he could do exactly that and in no time at all, Philip had crafted a brief message recounting what had occurred on the ship and sent the boy out to run while he stayed on the ship to formulate a plan.

He sat on his bunk and thought. Minutes turned into an hour, and one hour into two. Nothing came to mind as a good plan. There were upwards of thirty violent and angry escaped captives at large in New York City and the best plan that Philip could manage to devise was the feeble and obvious idea of going out and hunting them down. That didn't solve anything. That plan didn't say how they were to find them all, nor how to make sure that the city wasn't compromised. Not only did he have to think in terms of danger but also in regards to the city remaining ignorant of the reality of these creatures' existence.

Philip was still at a loss for ideas and inspiration when a slender shadow filled the doorway to his cabin. It was outlined by the afternoon sun behind it, so Philip couldn't tell who it was. He certainly wasn't expecting anyone. Instantly one dagger from his belt and the other from his sleeve, normal and silver respectively, shot into his hands and he leapt to his feet ready for a fight. He wasn't as rested as he would have liked following his midday, vampire-slaying exertions, but there was no time to waste on wishful thinking.

"Easy there," said an oddly familiar voice, and the slim shadow lifted its hands in a peaceful gesture as it took one step slowly backward and then another, "I'm not here t' fight." It retreated out onto the deck and Philip followed warily not putting either of his weapons away despite the assurance of peace from the voice.

Philip saw as they reached the full light of the afternoon sun that it was the gypsy half-breed, who had escaped, from the previous night.

"You," he said not able to think clearly enough. Philip tried to organize his thoughts; he had to keep his wits about him.

"Me," the lad bowed cheekily as he restated Philip's obvious conclusion. He was dressed the same, with his mismatched coat and breeches, scraggly hair, and plethora of charms and necklaces. However, he looked to have grown dirtier than the night before, as if he had been in another scuffle or two since Philip had last seen him. He also seemed paler and slightly more tired like the way a person looked when they were on the verge of getting sick, but not quite there yet.

Philip grunted, "You don't look so well. Hard times since I saw you last night?"

The half-breed got an angry look in his eye for the first time, "Ya' could say that," he drawled. Even during their fight last night Philip had not seen the youth get mad. He had only seemed excited and exhilarated by the encounter. Something had changed since their last meeting.

"What do you want?" Philip queried not dropping his guard one bit. He knew how fast this gypsy lad was and in his fatigued state, even the slightest lack of focus and concentration would be the end of him should his opponent cease being peaceful and decide to attack.

"To talk, to share some information." He paused and winked at Philip. "Knowledge I think you need. And then maybe we can work t'gether."

Philip was confused. What information did he need? He had learned of many mysteries today and he wanted answers to all of them. Which ones did the half-breed think that he, Philip, understood? He needed to keep him talking.

"I don't trust you," Philip put it bluntly. He had never been one for unnecessary tact or bandying words in useless banter. It was verbal frivolity. "What makes you think I would work with you?"

"Ahh, well, because you need me o'course," the half-breed responded, "Your partner's dead and gone to which I offer you my condolences. That means you'll be needing somebody to partner with you and stop *him*." He gave Philip a more serious look. "And you won't be able to do it alone."

Philip narrowed his eyes and kept his stance steady, ready to defend. He was a stark contrast to the way the gypsy lad leaned casually,

The Collector

comfortably against the mast. "How do I know that you didn't do this? You could have been angry about last night and decided to get revenge." Philip asked the obvious question blocking their ability to move forward. "I'll need proof that you're not responsible."

"An' ya won't get it, least not proof irrefutable. You'll have to take me at my word when I say I'm not the culprit of this fine mess, and trust me when I tell you that my word is always good." He peered at Philip from beneath a lock of hair as he emphasized the word, *always*.

Philip shook his head in disbelief, "And why would I do that? I don't know anything about you other than the fact that you sliced me up pretty good last night. That doesn't lend much weight at all to my being able or desiring to trust you." How could the gypsy expect him to trust a complete stranger? Let alone one whom Philip had been pursuing for charges that had been labeled in the Guild report as "extreme thievery," and who knew what else.

The lad stepped away from the mast and began pacing back and forth lithely, even in the act of walking, he displayed his incredible ability to move quickly, and effortlessly with a grace that Philip had rarely ever seen.

"Why you ask?" he began, "Might I remind you that last night you were the one attempting to capture me, an' not the other way around." It was a fair point and Philip noted it. The lad kept speaking, "Also you will have to trust me because I'm telling you the truth when I say that what he did to the captives that he released from your cargo hold, he did to me as well." The half-breed's face hardened as he finished, "And I want to fix that, not to mention get back what he stole."

Philip began trying to piece the parts of the whole together. Somebody had set his captives free and killed his partner. That was a fact. Somebody, an undefined *he*, had captured the lad and taken from him something of value. Not to mention that the mystery man had done something to the lad, which he allegedly had done to the rest of the escaped captives also. Philip didn't like the way this was going, but it sounded like a tale too far-fetched to create. Besides, if the gypsy really wanted revenge, he would have attacked by now.

"Okay," Philip spoke, "assuming I do believe you, I'll need a little more than what you've given me to strike up a temporary alliance." The lad cocked his head and lifted his eyebrows as if waiting for a question that he was not sure would come. Philip decided to continue.

"Well, for starters, what are you?" Philip asked.

"Why, I'm Irish o'course." The gypsy lad answered, doing a slight caper with his feet for effect.

Philip rolled his eyes and exhaled in frustration. "No, I mean *what* are you? I wouldn't have been ordered to Collect you if you weren't something special." Philip felt odd discussing the Guild's proceedings with a stranger and a former quarry, at that.

"Ahhhh, ya' mean, *who* am I?" the lad answered blinking with feigned innocence at avoiding the question a moment ago. "What a man is, is plain to see, but who," he opened his hands wide in an instructional flourish, "meaning his name and the essence of his being can be a much more complicated issue."

"Well?" Philip waited for the real response.

"The name's Beathan," Philip's potential ally inclined his head in formal introduction, "and I'm part fairy, part human, and a wee bit o' leprechaun way, way back on me ma's side o' the family."

His lilting brogue indicated that he might be telling the truth. It was certainly an Irish accent, and although half-breeds weren't extremely common, Philip had encountered them before. But a mix, however slight, of more than two races was something of which he had never heard. It was an oddity, but one that he guessed didn't really matter in the grand scheme of things. Fairy. The fairy folk were much akin to their human counterparts, the gypsy, and traveling kin of Europe. Indeed many of the gypsy customs and traditions had been adopted from their early encounters with the Fairy Kind.

Fairies were clever, crafty, and often deceptive. However, they were not on the list of most violent or malevolent of creatures, falling more in the category of dangerously mischievous. It was a fine line, no doubt, but a line to which Philip would have to cling if he did decide to ally himself with Beathan.

Beathan finished his introduction and inquired of Philip the same thing. "And now may I ask what about you? Who are ya?"

"My name is Philip, and I'm just a man," Philip responded warily.

The Collector

"No, no." The half-fairy shook his head in disapproval. Philip's answer deemed unfit for some reason. "That's not it."

"What do you mean?" asked Philip.

"I mean," Beathan paused for emphasis, "that you're mighty strong for a man who looks to be as slender as you. T'aint hardly natural."

Indeed, he would have realized that after their skirmish the night before. Where to begin? Philip rarely had to explain his strength to humans, since he concealed it well from them. He was not in the business of detailing his history to his quarries, and an explanation of his strength had never really been asked of him except by James. His dead partner had been the only one alive, other than Mr. Astori, who had known the truth of the origins of Philip's inhuman strength.

Philip studied him carefully, weighing whether it would give away an advantage to disclose the information, and then finally nodded in acquiescence. He needed to build a working relationship with the gypsy lad, however tenuous it might be. Philip knew that he was not going to get to the bottom of this without help. Besides, someone of Beathan's talents might come in handy to have around.

Philip responded in his usual succinct manner. "Some troll's blood was added to mine when I was a boy for the purpose of its healing properties. The strength was an unforeseen side effect of which my parents were unaware until I grew older." Philip studied his new ally closely, looking for any hint of emotion or thought on his face. It would help to gauge him better if he knew what the gypsy was thinking. However, Beathan kept his features closed as he waited for more of Philip's story, so Philip continued. "I keep it hidden, when possible, to avoid notice and unwanted questions. Other than that, I'm all human," Philip finished with a wry twist of his mouth, which he supposed some people might interpret as a smile.

"That's it?" Beathan remarked with feigned incredulity. "I expected more of a tale than that. Maybe a story of woe an' wonder woven t'gether into a tapestry of your history." He flashed a genuine grin at Philip, the kind of smile that was hard for a person to refuse. As much as Philip tried to guard his emotions, he found that he liked this witty, impulsive half-breed. He would still proceed with caution, but he felt enjoyment and even a measure of trust growing.

Mathias G. B. Colwell

In response to his intuition, Philip stuck both the knives he still held in his hands back into their places of concealment—one to his belt and the other to his boot. Philip decided to volunteer just a portion more of the story.

"Very well," Philip said and pretended to be put out at having to explain more of his past. "I was ill as a child. From the moment I was born there was something wrong with my health."

Beathan smiled a small smile as he picked up on the nuances of Philip's feigned frustration at being called to speak more. The half-breed leaned back against the mast again in his familiar stance of casualness. In truth it was good to talk, Philip realized. As much as he didn't know this Beathan, he felt he could trust him, perhaps more than he had trusted any new acquaintance in a long while. At the very least Philip knew that the fairy meant him no harm for now. That would have to suffice, seeing as they both were counting on an alliance, a partnership of sorts, to form and propel them to their desired outcomes.

"When I was still a child," Philip recounted the tale his parents had told him on a number of occasions before they had passed away, "no more than six years of age, I finally succumbed to what appeared to be the last of the many infections and infirmities of my short youth." He paused for a breath and then continued. "I was on my death bed but my parents had not yet given up hope." Philip watched as even his limited tale intrigued Beathan and the fairy lad's eyes began to light up as a person's eyes do when the theatrics and dramatics of storytelling carve out a piece of the past and bring it to life.

"At that point in time we were living in the north of Europe, the Nordic lands, where there are many beings other than just humans inhabiting the wilderness." Philip continued, "Some of these creatures possess different talents and abilities, or natural properties."

He knew that Beathan understood what he meant. His ally's lightning speed was exactly that, along with any other fairy talents he possessed. Philip was certain that the lad possessed more abilities than just speed. Most fairy folk, even half-breeds, were able to manipulate magic to a certain degree, if not to the extent that an accomplished witch or magician might be able. However, one thing he did know was that the

The Collector

intentions of most fairy folk were far less harmful than a witch or magician, often stemming from where they derived their power.

Witches often derived their power from a darker magic, thriving on pain and despair, and evil of the worst kind. Many magicians were the same, those not posing as cheap charlatans that is. Fairies often drew their limited magic from a purer source, the very land around them. They also tended to be most powerful in the land of their inheritance, the source of their birth, their life, and purpose. If Beathan's own explanation was true, then it stood to reason that he was much less powerful here in America than he would be in his homeland of Ireland.

Beathan nodded that he did see where Philip's recounting of his past was going. "Hence the trolls," he completed the idea Philip had begun introducing.

"Yes," Philip agreed, "My parents were accomplished enough Collectors to catch and draw blood from their quarry, a troll. The medical instrument barely could pierce the skin, but with work they managed to puncture through." Philip thought of his parents fondly and rather proudly. They had been an accomplished couple within the Guild. "They then injected the blood into me and waited to see what would happen. The legends said that trolls had many abilities, among which were being impervious to magic, having immense strength, and of course, having the ability to heal quickly. The last trait, which allowed for quick healing, was the benefit my parents were seeking from the blood transfusion." He trailed off as his story drew to a close.

"There isn't much more to tell than that," Philip finished up. "I don't know whether the blood itself was enough to catalyze my return to health, or if my parents had access to a magician who initiated the healing process with a magical catalyst of sorts." Philip thought of Mr. Astori and how it was possible that he had played a part in Philip's recovery, although he did not technically have that confirmation. He continued, "All I know is that my young body healed and my parents were ecstatic. Not only did I not experience such a lack of health as I had before, but also, as I grew older and matured, it became clear that the blood of the trolls had mixed with mine in a greater way than they had anticipated." The untamable cry of the mountains and the wild was truly more a part of him than he had ever really admitted, Philip reflected as he spoke.

Philip headed off the argument that he anticipated. "I know, I know," he placated a non-existent disagreement with his hands, "I am very thin and not very hairy." The next bit came out in a flood of words. "So you ask yourself how could my blood have possibly mixed more with the trolls than we thought? It was the strength that made us realize it. I grew stronger than any human my age, and as I grew older, my strength increased until even my parents had to concede that it would be well for me to hide it, lest the Guild themselves grew too suspicious."

Now Beathan smirked. "Hiding your ability from the very organization for which you work." He chuckled and clapped his hands as if it was great humor.

"No," Philip responded, his blood heating suddenly, "not from everyone. There are those within the Guild that know." Philip thought of his deceased partner James, and his mentor Mr. Astori. "But we keep the knowledge from the greater public, both for my benefit and for theirs."

"Easy, easy," Beathan shushed him still grinning, "T'was only a joke. I meant no harm. Truly I did not." It was true; Philip could see no malice in his gaze. The lad really was as light-hearted a person as Philip had ever met. It appeared he could see the joke in every situation.

Nevertheless, it had touched a nerve inside Philip. This wasn't the first time he had contemplated his choice to work for the Guild. He had been born into it, raised by Collectors, but there were moments when he wondered if he could really be considered human anymore. If he was being completely honest with himself, were he to describe a person in the exact same condition as himself to another member of the Guild, he would refer to them as a half-breed, part human, part something else. The thought alone was enough to question his ideals if he let it. He usually avoided it, and planted his feet and his morals on the firm rock that was the truth of how he chased and locked away dangerous beings. He told himself that that was all that mattered. He didn't hurt people so he was different than the variety of supernatural creatures he spent his life pursuing. Yet, the thought that perhaps he had chosen to ally himself with the wrong side of this conflict could never quite be erased from the back of his mind. It didn't help either, that in recent years corruption had

The Collector

begun to take hold inside the Guild. The stories of creatures being sold into a private investor's personal menagerie, or being released by the Collector for a profit were increasingly more common. Even the occurrence of a stricter, senior member such as Mr. Astori breaking the guidelines and sending a Collector such as Philip on a solo mission as had happened earlier today, were more frequent than in times past. It was a changing world, and it appeared that the Guild was evolving as well, though Philip could not see it as good. These thoughts were a slippery slope, and Philip often chose not to think them. It was easier to focus on the good things that he was certain he did, than allow himself to fall in the dangerous abyss of questioning the morality of his life's decisions.

He waved a placating hand to Beathan, showing he understood that it had been an attempt at humor to which he had overreacted. Philip was normally a calm, steady individual, but even the most stable of people had deep-seated issues that when touched upon could reveal a raw, open sore. This was one of those things for Philip—an unsettled question floating, bouncing around his subconscious.

The pitter-patter of small, bare feet sounded on the gangplank and Philip swiveled towards the entry point of his ship. He loosed a dagger from his belt and had it in his hand, ready to throw, before he realized that the sound must be Stephen returning from his couriering. Sure enough, the boy came into view and Philip shoved the knife back in its place at his waist. He chanced a swift look at Beathan and was pleased to see that nearly the same reaction of wariness and even a twinge of fear were fading from the fairy's face as he saw the child coming in their direction. Philip could tell that he was not the only one with frayed nerves after the proceedings of the day.

"Well, lad you've returned in good time." Philip tried to speak as cheerfully as he could. "You must have run the entire way." Sure enough the boy looked tired. He was panting the way someone did when winded after a long run.

"Yes sir," the boy paused as he gulped air, "I went to each location you gave me." Stephen stated it as matter-of-factly as one could when struggling for their breath. He seemed determined to make up for his earlier bout of hiding by adopting what he had decided was an adult practicality of speech.

Mathias G. B. Colwell

Philip nodded in approval. "And," he leaned his head toward the boy, drawing out the word in question form. Stephen gulped, his boyish nerves showing through his newly acquired adult façade, but didn't respond. Philip decided to go on with the obvious train of thought. "So you delivered the messages," it was a statement not a question yet, "and what did the Guild members say?"

This time the boy swallowed his nervousness and answered, "No sir. I did not deliver the messages."

Philip was confused now. The boy wasn't making any sense. "And why not?" he asked Stephen, exasperation beginning to show at having to pull information out of the boy.

An Irish voice answered quietly in what Philip would have described as a melancholy, sadly toned whisper. "Because they are all dead."

Stephen looked to Beathan and nodded grateful to not have been forced to say such a horrible thing himself. "Yes sir, that's exactly it." He dry washed his hands. "Well that is, not completely, I guess. Truth of it is three of them were dead when I found them, but the last, Mr. Astori, was nowhere to be found. His manservant said that he had been out of contact since morning. That he was missing."

Missing. Something prickled at the back of Philip's mind and he pondered the facts as Beathan and Stephen shared a greeting after being introduced to one another by Philip. The Guild members dead. James dead. Somehow through all of that, Mr. Astori was the only one not dead. Something didn't add up. He was almost onto it, the idea forming in the front of his thoughts, the way a word hangs on the tip of a tongue, when Stephen interrupted his thinking.

"Master Philip, Sir, I nearly forgot," the boy piped, his voice cracking. Philip regretfully let the thoughts subside. There would be another moment to figure this out. There had to be.

"What lad?" he asked with slight impatience.

The boy pulled a bouquet of flowers out from behind his back where they had been tucked into his belt. They were a small, pitiful handful of winter blooms. All of them blue pansies accompanied by one red rose. Philip sucked in his breath and alarm bells chimed in his skull.

56

The Collector

Somebody knew. This was beyond bad. Alayna was in danger because somebody knew they were connected.

Beathan saw immediately the effect the flowers had on Philip, and cocked his head silently, an unspoken question, his shaggy blondish hair falling in front of the raised side of his head. The question didn't go unnoticed to Philip but he chose not to answer it just yet.

"Where did you get those, boy?" he asked fearing the answer.

Stephen seemed unaware of the rise in tension since he had pulled free the flowers from his belt. "A messenger delivered them to me just as I was about to board the ship. He said they were for the owner of the vessel." The boy seemed a bit confused at the question. "That's you sir. You're the owner."

Philip kept his silence, thinking. Finally Beathan asked the question out loud, "Who are they from, Philip?"

Philip closed his eyes painfully and shook his head in remorse as he answered, "Alayna."

"Your lass?" The Celtic fairy asked lightly. Again cocking his head in question as Philip regretfully affirmed it with a grimace and a nod. "I'm not quite certain what's amiss with a few flowers, mate," Beathan queried, "could ya' fill me in on where the trouble lies?"

Philip acquiesced and they began discussing the private details of his budding romance with the beautiful Miss Oakdale.

"I met Alayna last year during our Collections," Philip started as Stephen, Beathan and he sat down. "James and I had spent the previous two months working our way north from the tip of Florida all the way up the Atlantic coast." Philip decided to be blunt and not dodge details. "We bagged everything from vampires, to monstrous apes, to werewolves and murderous fairies."

Beathan's eyes hardened at the mention of fairies but he kept silent, listening to the story, and perhaps as hard as it might be for him to hear, there were indeed some fairy folk near as dangerous as the more bloodthirsty sort of creatures. Witches and magicians weren't the only ones with magic, nor the only ones occasionally known to abandon the lighter side of magic and delve into its darker, more damaging cousin, the occult.

Philip ignored Beathan's rare scowl and continued, "As we were about to finish up our mission and head back to England, much like we were supposed to do today, we opted to make one last stop in the New York area as we had heard rumors of a 'goatman' that had been deceiving his way into some of the farm houses in the countryside." He paused to look at his audience and slipped slightly into teaching mode, which was a common default whenever he spoke with Stephen.

"If you are at all aware of the enigmatic, then you know that Fauns are commonly mistaken for some kind of goat person." Philip clarified, "It was probably a faun who had somehow made its way to American shores unnoticed and was taking advantage of poor families in rural areas." Philip didn't feel the need to explain in front of the boy what he meant by a faun 'taking advantage' of families. The boy was still somewhat innocent and he didn't want to cloud his head with the rougher side of the Collector's job. That rough side sometimes entailed dealing with creatures like fauns, who were characteristically more devious than almost any creature, spinning a web of lies and deceit that was nothing short of its own evil kind of spell. Not all creatures could procreate without humans. Fauns were one of those creatures, and a particularly nasty kind at that.

Philip could tell Beathan understood what he had been hinting at as once again the fairy's eyes darkened with dislike at what he was hearing. Only this time Philip was certain it was the faun's debauchery of which he was questioning the morality, not Philip's penchant for capturing creatures.

The story went on uninterrupted. "James and I dealt with the threat to the countryside and as we were heading back into the city we stopped in hopes of refreshment at the house of a young lady, living alone on the outskirts of New York."

Philip sighed pleasantly as he thought of her and then kept speaking, "Alayna's family had all passed years before in a fever that had swept the area and she was living alone in the cottage." He smiled as he remembered. "She was prettier than a spring morning and more joyful than a songbird that had just been freed from its cage."

Beathan smiled as he listened to Philip describe his courtship with Alayna, how he had gone back in secret the next night, not telling even

The Collector

James, and begun his wooing of the lovely girl. Philip told of how they had taken walks when he was in the area, corresponded when he was off in different parts of America or England, and how at last he had even revealed to her the true nature of his job. He had told her they must keep their affair secret.

"Why did it need to be secret, Sir?" asked Stephen who had been sucked into the tale.

Philip grinned somewhat ruefully. "Because my boy, Beathan here," and he jerked his head at the half-breed, "isn't the first of my quarries to make a clean getaway and avoid capture. The things I chase don't always take it too kindly, being hunted." Philip pursed his lips thoughtfully and then spoke. "I thought it was safer if we kept our romance secret. It would protect her from unnecessary dangers." Nobody had known about her, not even James.

"So tell me about the flowers, then," Beathan suggested, "we don't have all day to reminisce about your love affair." He nudged Philip playfully and Philip was surprised at how natural the fairy's companionship was already beginning to feel.

"Right you are," Philip agreed. "The flowers were a signal to meet. All blue for any time of convenience, all blue with a red rose for an urgent matter." He sighed as the problem at hand brought reality crashing back into focus. The stroll down the last year's memory lane had been nice, but possibly a waste of precious time.

Beathan squinted at the flowers. "Well then, it's an urgent matter, that doesn't necessarily mean something's gone wrong." The half-breed was yet again trying to look at the bright side.

"True," Philip conceded, "however, I cannot think for a moment it is coincidence that today of all days she sends me an urgent message to meet. Besides, we had decided upon morning glories as our means of communication. That she chose to send pansies makes me fear that someone had forced her to reach out to me and she is trying to warn me the only way she knows how—by deliberately sending something to me that is outside of the normal."

Indeed Philip was afraid that whoever was behind the haphazard and sinister events of today had somehow managed to find out about Alayna and was using her as a pawn.

"I must go to her," he proclaimed at last, "whether it is a trap or not, I cannot wait to find out. I believe this turn of events is directly tied to what must be done to solve our current problems." Philip wasn't sure how he knew, but he had a hunch that some answers and possibly clarity would occur when they reached Alayna's.

"I'll go with you o' course," Beathan said. Philip nodded in thanks and agreement. Alayna's involvement in the day's events, just now, had changed things. Philip couldn't afford to question the half-breed's motives any longer. The time to act had arrived. Sometimes a man had to take a risk and pay the consequences for his actions later, for good or for ill, because the price of not taking any action at all was a much greater gamble in and of itself. Philip supposed he could always attempt to Collect Beathan when this was all over if trusting the fairy turned out to be a poor decision. Hopefully it wouldn't have to come to that.

Stephen bravely stood up with them, as they made ready to depart. "I'll go with you too, Sir."

"No, you won't lad," Philip responded gently but firmly. "It's too dangerous. You wait here one day. If by tomorrow evening I haven't returned, then I want you to make your way to a Mr. Thomas Deardy, he owns the pub 'Lucky Lucy,' down at the end of the wharf. Do you know him?" Stephen nodded his head up and down, that yes he did. "Good," Philip said, "he's a friend, and will set you up with passage back to England and the Guild. Just tell him you're my apprentice and he'll look out for you. A good friend he is." And with that he and Beathan made ready to leave and walked their way down the gangplank to the wagon. Stephen watched them go forlornly from the deck of the ship.

"Tomorrow evening mind you," he called back to the boy as they reached the grey stone of the wharf, "not an hour longer." And with that they arrived at the wagon.

"Horses alone will be faster," Beathan suggested, all business for once, "an' easier to negotiate through a crowd if it proves necessary. Not to mention they aren't cumbersome like this whale of a land-ship ya' have here," he finished slapping the wagon humorously, deviating from the uncharacteristic solemnity of a moment before.

Philip agreed and they unhitched the horses. Philip also grabbed as much weapons and supplies from his wagon as a shoulder-sack could

The Collector

carry while Beathan laughed at his preparations. In Philip's mind it never hurt to be prepared and there were a host of angry, escaped creatures out there that would love to get a hold of Philip just now. Beathan understood, Philip knew, but he had also begun to realize that the half-breed lived his life in a different realm than Philip and most other people. Danger was excitement in Beathan's world, and caution and preparation were considered boring. He was much like James in a way, providing a lightness to balance Philip's serious, plan-oriented nature. It was strange that so soon after his death, James' position as partner to Philip would be filled by somebody with such similar tendencies. Philip supposed that things had a way of ending up as they should. Fate, he had learned, had a funny sense of humor.

Chapter Five

They rode the horses away from the ship at a swift trot. The wharf gave way to crowded streets, the afternoon sun piercing the clouds, sending rays of light glinting off metal pipe stems in the mouths of men going about their business, and reflecting off the bolts and metal bits on horses and carriages. It was crowded, but they wound their way as quickly as they could through the throng of people.

Philip, not for the first time, wondered what it would be like to live the way the vast majority of these people did, oblivious to the reality of danger swirling within their midst. Witches and vampires, werewolves and fauns, among many other wicked beings had been freed earlier today from Philip's ship. They would have had to pass through the city, either to leave or possibly to build a nest for themselves. New York City was about to become one of the least pleasant places to live in all of the Atlantic shore. Not in all of Philip's years as a Collector had he heard of a mass escape such as the one that had been engineered today. It was shameful that it had happened on his watch. He tried to keep his head clear of what he knew could be debilitating self-blame. Crippling one's self with doubt was not the way to go about cleaning up a mess; making up for his mistakes, and solving whatever venomous riddle that had reared its ugly head today, was at the top of his list of things to do.

Crowded city streets, full of smoke from chimneys wafting low as a cold breeze pushed them uncharacteristically low, melted into oblivion as they entered a wooded area just outside the city. The sounds of the city faded and then grew silent. Alayna's cottage was only a short

The Collector

distance from the city limits, but with the way the afternoon light was fading and turning into evening, Philip was eager to get there. It would be good to get inside cover and out of such an exposed position. He was as accustomed as anyone could be to the supernatural, but today was different than normal, even for Philip. There were too many dangerous creatures loose in one place for him to feel safe.

"So, why don't you start talking?" Philip suggested as they rode. "If we really are to work together, I'll need to know what you know. For starters, who took you and what did he do to you?"

"Magic is what he did," Beathan answered as nonchalantly as only a non-human being could do, "and about as vile a magic as I ever saw. Not a once did I see such evil magic on me fair, green isle." His face sobered up more than normal, his usually bright smile disappearing beneath furrowed eyes and a disgusted sneer. "It'll be the death of me if we don't catch up with him and rectify it."

Philip narrowed his eyes and said, "Explain." One word was all that was needed. The half-breed spun the tale of the last half-day or so, leaving out no details. It appeared that the very same night after he had given Philip the slip, he had wandered aimlessly, just trying to avoid notice and stay clear of trouble. Apparently, even for him, the fight with Philip had been enough excitement for one night. It hadn't worked out that simply though, as he had turned a corner and in his fatigued and weakened state had been taken unawares. He described the encounter to Philip.

"T'was like I turned the corner into an invisible net, me arms and limbs tangled in the air, the likes o' which only magic can accomplish." He shook his head regretfully. "I'm not weak of mind nor will, nor body, but as that old magician jigged my way with his cane, I felt me insides melt, an' me mind wobble and blur under the web o' his spell."

Philip listened carefully, like an investigator hoping to pick up every clue possible from a crime scene he had not witnessed. He stayed silent and let Beathan finish his story.

The half-breed carried on in typical, wordy fashion. "I don't rightly know what that magician did to me," he commented honestly, "but t'was a bonding of sorts. After the spell was laid, I could *feel* him and he me."

Mathias G. B. Colwell

Beathan shivered slightly as if that experience had been too much even for a free-spirited, adventurer like him.

"Like he was within me. Not controlling me mind ya," he clarified, as they rode under a copse of trees, the dirt road beneath the horses hooves thudding dully as they galloped, "but as though he was aware of me every move an' thought. T'was an unkindly experience, to have another's mind inside yer own."

The story went on; Beathan told how the old magician had watched him struggle futilely in his spell-web before stealing a bracelet from his wrist and disappearing, practically into thin air. Philip didn't disbelieve Beathan, or think that he was exaggerating. He had witnessed enough witches and magicians perform wilder things than that. Beathan struggled to explain the next part, however.

"After he left I figured I'd better lay even lower, an' plan what to do," he shrugged. "Folks like me," Philip wasn't sure if he was referring to the gypsy or the fairy in him, "we don't like to attract notice. Avoid it when at all possible." Beathan grimaced wryly. "I'd attracted more notice in one night, between you and that foul magician, than I had in longer 'n I can recall."

Philip understood what he meant. Most likely, he was a thief of sorts, a conjurer of tricks with a small amount of magic to deceive people and make the means to stay on the road and keep travelling. It fit with his gypsy, fairy, and even his leprechaun blood if that portion of his personal history was true. It also explained why he would want to avoid notice. Dishonest types frequently preferred as little attention as possible. Philip pulled his mind away from its current path and reminded himself that the half-breed was now the only help he had at the moment, a partner of sorts. It was hard to erase decades of stereotypes and prejudice, however. Philip once again kept quiet and waited for the telling to draw to its close.

Beathan spouted out more of his tale, his mouth running nearly as fast as his feet. It was nearly as hard to understand him, as it was to catch him at times; his Irish accent seemed to grow thicker as he grew more distressed.

The Collector

"I ran off utilizing me gifts and abilities but I quickly realized something was amiss." He shook his head in frustration. "T'was as if he managed to harness me powers and take them for his own strength."

Philip scrunched his forehead in confusion and Beathan saw that Philip didn't really understand what he was implying.

"When I use my gifts—speed, agility, me slight trickery an' spell work—I normally feel fine, but not so now. When I try and use them now, I can still make them work but it feels different. I can literally sense the energy and magic seeping out of me and going someplace else."

The fairy flourished a hand and a rose appeared out of thin air. Philip wasn't sure if it was the small bit of magic he was alluding to or slight-of-the-hand. In this case, it must be magic to be an ability he reasoned.

"That is unsettling indeed," Philip responded. Just the thought of something being able to sap the strength and energy of a being was uncanny. It was not something of which he had ever heard, a black magic to be certain.

"Wait!" Philip interjected, "I had a confrontation with two vampires earlier today, one was adult and fought well until suddenly it lost all strength and shriveled up. The same happened to the weaker, young one after barely struggling." He stared at Beathan and then moved his gaze onto the wooded forest they were entering. "Do you think that is the end result of the," he paused struggling to find a word to describe the magic used on Beathan, "power of which you speak?"

"It is certainly possible," replied Beathan with conviction, "T'would be a strange coincidence were it not related." Beathan rode on in silence a moment longer, the evening sun behind him creating a shadowed face as if he were cloaked in a hood. He proposed another even more unsettling prospect. "I believe whoever this magician is, he has found a way to harness our power, bond us, and as we wither and die with its use, he acquires it and gains strength." Beathan brooded another moment in dark thought. "It is possible he gains even youth from this exchange."

It made sense in a terrifying way to Philip who had, only a half day past, watched two supernatural beings shrivel, and what Philip now understood must have been, age directly in front of him. If there was a magician that could steal youth and strength, then he must be stopped at all costs. There was no telling what might happen if he were allowed to exercise this power unchecked for too much longer. Already he grew powerful, and if he had created this same link or bond with the escaped creatures, which it was fair to conclude he had, then there was a small army of beasts adding to his power right now as they rode.

"You mentioned he stole a bracelet from you?" Philip dug deeper for more information.

Beathan looked reluctant to speak on it, a reticence that was odd from such a freely spoken individual. He answered nonetheless, "Ay, he did. It's mine, an' I'll have it back," he said fiercely. Philip was reminded by the tone of his voice and dangerous gleam in his eye that his newfound partner was much more dangerous and capable of violent response than his deceptively charming attitude proclaimed.

"What is so special about that particular bracelet?" Philip eyed askance at the rest of Beathan's assortment of jewelry on his neck, arms, fingers and even his ears. Beathan kept his mouth shut and looked like he was about to refuse to answer. Philip opened his mouth to react to the lack of information forthcoming from his new partner, when a roar ripped the evening stillness.

The woods were not thick, and the fading light still penetrated from the sky to the road, casting long, thin shadows of trees and creating a twilight gloom that clouded the sight. It was just at the verge of being difficult to see their surroundings. It was as if the world's Creator was painting purplish, broad, brush-strokes across the sky and land. It was normal Collecting circumstances for Philip. Another roar pierced the air and then mid-sound, it morphed into a deep, rough howl of sorts. The noise was what Philip imagined it would sound like if more than one creature joined into one body.

Beathan saw the grimace on Philip's face and simply answered, "Later," to Philip's prior question about the uniqueness of the stolen bracelet before continuing on to ask his own question. The half-breed asked, "Philip, what manner of creature pursues us?" He smirked in his casual, reckless fashion and waited for a response. It appeared that very little was able to dampen the fairy's spirits. The same fearsome growl cascaded through the sky to their backs, sounding closer than it had before.

The Collector

"It's called a Wendigo," Philip volunteered more information, "and it's one of the few creatures that is native to this land. It's probably the worst of what was on our ship and set loose," Philip began breathlessly, the onward rush of the horses requiring more effort than he had anticipated. "Powerful, fast, vicious, and with a bite that can do more than just kill you even if you do escape."

Not many creatures could claim origins in America. However there were some creatures, like the Wendigo, that had a history in America far older than the first arrival of European immigrants on this soil. And a creation in the habitat of its origination was often much more powerful there than when it was Collected and removed. Philip didn't really understand completely, all he knew was that the connection between a being and its land of birth was mystical and enigmatic.

"Right," Beathan grinned impudently, "I like the way this adventure is beginning to sound." He winked at Philip, "Well, if ya' were able to catch it once, I don't see how we won't be able to dispose of it, or at the very least, evade it with meself and me own expertise added t' the equation."

Philip shook his head and rolled his eyes, trying his best to adopt a similar, casual manner to the situation the way Beathan had. It was pointless. Philip had never been able to erase the fact that his nerves seemed to tighten up almost excruciatingly before and during a fight. Other Collectors got loose and relaxed claiming that relieving the tension was crucial to survival. Philip on the other hand had always embraced the nerves and used them as fuel. He did so once again, resolving to be himself, as it had worked for him countless times.

"Well," Beathan said, as another half-howl reached their ears yet again, closer than the previous. "Just how dangerous is it?"

"Very," Philip responded solemnly. He hauled on the reins of the horses, and Beathan turned his horse around in surprise at Philip's actions. "It's big. It took everything James and I had to offer to capture it the first time. We nearly didn't. That collection might have ended in utter failure if we hadn't been blessed with the fortune of it being full daylight, a time when the beast operates at the least of its potential." It was not so now, in the twilight of the day.

Philip answered the unspoken question. "We cannot outrun it, and even if we could, I would not lead a thing of such malice even one step closer to the door of Alayna's home. We make our stand here." The two of them reined in their horses in unison.

Beathan appraised him and seemed to find a new aspect of Philip that he hadn't seen before, a protector of those he loved as opposed to just a man who captured things for a living. The fairy nodded his agreement, and as the sounds of the beast grew closer he asked, "What exactly is this beast? I can't rightly say I've heard of it, seeing as I am just a visitor t' these fine shores."

"This monster is not one that many hear of outside of the Northeast of this continent," Philip began. "Some call it 'The Spirit of Lonely Places,' others the Wendigo. Either way it is a right fit to handle. Took nearly all of James and my skill and daring to capture it."

He shook his head at the memory of such a terrible fight. Philip continued, his left knee almost touching Beathan's as they sat astride their horses, calmly waiting for the Wendigo's ominous arrival. "Imagine a mixture between a werewolf, a troll and an ape-man." Philip steeled his heart and mind as best he could. Lesser men had been known to quake at the approach of a Wendigo; he did not fault them much. "It is devilish in nature, feeding on the flesh of the living, and children especially, whenever possible. The natives of this land have had a long history of legend and myth telling of its existence."

Philip took a breath before proceeding. "James and I tracked it into Algonquin land, a native tribe, and took it down before it could do any more harm to their people. To be completely honest, it isn't a creature to which I am extremely familiar. I am relying mostly on legends and native storytellers for my information."

Beathan understood and queried further, "What, might I ask, do these native tale-weavers say?"

Philip unhooked the crossbow he had slung over his shoulder and loaded a silver bolt into it. The silver bolts were most effective with werewolves, but they would slow this creature down also, even if it wasn't the silver property itself that was a factor. Beathan freed up two knives from hiding places on his body, and twirled them idly as he waited for Philip to answer.

The Collector

"Legend around these parts say that they weren't always beasts, that their origins are human," Philip said quietly.

"Akin to the lychan ya' mentioned earlier," Beathan said keenly. He knew more than he let on at times. Lychan was another name for the werewolf family however, its use was less common.

Philip nodded in agreement. "Yes, and their bite is said to have similar effects. I don't know if the bite changes you or if something more is required as well to do so, but what I do know is that the effects of the bite would be undesirable."

His partner quirked an Irish eyebrow in question, his typical and mischievous smile in place, and Philip continued.

"The bite, or change, however it happens, makes you hunger for human flesh. It turns you into a cannibal or something like that, before eventually transforming your physical form in accordance with the changes to your appetites." Philip rushed his explanation, as far down the road the creature came into view. It was indeed a monstrosity. The thing was twice the size of a man, and had powerfully yoked arms in the manner of apes, or even trolls. It ran alternating on two legs, then bounding leaps on all fours, almost as if it couldn't decide whether it was humanoid or beast. Philip had no question, whatever the origins; this thing was now a beast, a thing of complete evil.

"Cannibal, eh?" The half-breed responded thoughtfully, "Well, I'll make sure t' avoid his maw," he laughed and nudged Philip jokingly. Philip didn't laugh. "Oh, come on mate, if this is to be the end of me, I mean to go out in high style." He picked at his faded green coat sarcastically, poking fun at his haphazard apparel, "And with a grin on me face and a laugh on me tongue." He slapped Philip's shoulder encouragingly and booted his horse a step towards the beast in anxious anticipation for the clash at hand. Philip wished he could adopt the same carefree attitude.

The Wendigo had closed ground fast and was only about fifty yards away now. Brutish features covered in coarse hair met a thick neck and thick shoulders. The hair thinned at the shoulders and grew patchy and scarce in a disgusting manner as it spread down the ape-like arms. Its core was like the arms, a chest of sparse hair and a bigger belly on it than you would have guessed by the pace at which it was moving. Its legs changed back into the thick hair akin to its head and neck, turning its legs into a forest of blackness. Pointed ears of a canine look, protruded from the sides of its head and swiveled sharply and often. Philip had no doubt that it caught every sound.

"Avoid the teeth," Philip muttered to himself and Beathan grinned at him. When it was about thirty-five yards away, Philip sighted crossbow on the beast and pulled the trigger. The familiar recoil of the bow against his shoulder was a comfort and the bolt flew true. It was a streaking ray of silver in the near darkness, burying itself in the left shoulder of the onrushing creature. The Wendigo jerked backward a moment yet barely slowed its pace as it continued.

"How do you think it found us?" Beathan asked.

Philip shrugged as he loaded one more bolt hurriedly, hoping to get another shot off before it was too tight of quarters and answered, "Must've caught my scent. It's probably got a vendetta against me. I can't imagine it's been bagged more than one time in its life, so it's probably enraged at being captured."

He let the second, and last, bolt fly, and sure enough, it hit home, the right arm of the beast recoiling from impact. The Wendigo was now close enough to see its facial features. It let out a scream of rage, tore the bolt out of its arm with its teeth and then spat the thing to the side as it continued its melee course towards them. Hopefully, a bolt to either side of its body would slow it down some, however Philip wasn't counting on it, as the beast didn't appear to have slowed a bit.

"We must split," Beathan urged, and he sprung left on his horse as Philip guided his right and the beast charged between them, swinging its paws wildly, claws missing Philip's head by only a hair. He felt the breath of wind rush by him and spun around to face the creature as Beathan did the same.

The Wendigo roared and gnashed its teeth, saliva and drool slathering out of its mouth in copious amounts. Indeed Philip did not wish to find out what should happen if those jaws closed about any part of his body.

Beathan leapt from his horse and to Philip's surprise, sprinted towards the thing. Philip couldn't let his partner bear the brunt of the attack alone, so he urged his horse forward.

The Collector

Beathan engaged the creature, and swung a flurry of slicing blows with his daggers, all the while dodging the mighty swings of the beast's paws. He inflicted a number of gashes upon the creature's forearms, but they only seemed to infuriate it more than cause any real harm. Philip pulled a knife from his boot and let it loose aiming for the creature's eye. He missed and the knife clattered harmlessly off the Wendigo's forehead, hilt first. It roared and turned its attention toward Philip, ignoring Beathan for a moment. It lunged at Philip and he only barely managed to direct his horse away from the thing's grasp. Beathan dashed in close and slashed at the beast's hamstring and in a reaction quicker than Philip would have imagined possible, it swatted behind itself with one massive paw and sent Beathan flying head over heels into a tree on the side of the trail. He shook his head to try to clear it before working his way back to his feet. Philip once again bore the brunt of the assault of the Wendigo. The thing paused to throw back its head and bellow in a primal fashion before advancing on Philip.

"Kill," it muttered in a garbled attempt at language. Philip knew the beast might possibly have been human, but hearing it speak now only further reinforced how far from a man it now was. The tongue swallowed up its words and that single word was the only one Philip could understand out of a string of growling partial words and sounds.

It advanced menacingly and Philip ducked a massive paw swipe, squirming in close for a few body strikes with his own powerful fists. He might not be as strong as the Wendigo, but Philip had come to accept that neither was he purely human, since his own genetic make-up was mixed with that of a troll. Philip's brown hair and thin, plain features of a man could not erase the fact that he was different. Teaming up with Beathan and seeing the 'humanistic' side of his quarries made him realize just how normal some of them could truly be. It forced him to shorten the gap he had created in his mind between himself and the creatures he had hunted. Whether by choice or by action he was only part human and there was no way around it.

It might have been awkward to punch from horseback, if the beast had not been so tall. He delivered a strong underhanded blow to the Wendigo's ribs and another and another, and for the first time it groaned in pain as it felt the wrath of Philip's own might, the strength infused by a troll's blood so many, long years ago. However, promptly after its groan of pain it recovered and swatted Philip with the back of its hand hard enough to send him reeling and his horse dancing backwards out of range. Philip thanked his stars that the horse was smart enough to do that. He dangled sideways, nearly falling from the saddle, the only thing keeping him atop the horse were his feet wedged in the stirrups.

Beathan saw that Philip was drawing the whole of the beast's attention and managed to reach his feet to begin creeping up from the back. Groggily, Philip noticed a strange occurrence. Through the mental fog of battle, he saw the Wendigo's fur was slowly but surely turning to silver. It took a step towards Philip and then another and still Philip couldn't shake the fog in his brain that was a result of the blow he had just suffered. If this was to be the end he thought vaguely then he was just glad Alayna wasn't there to see it.

The Wendigo sensed Philip's inability to recover quickly from the monster's powerful retaliatory strike. It leaned in with his mouth open. Fangs of all shapes, sizes and colors could be seen, dripping wet with the foulest smelling saliva Philip had ever seen. Just when he thought the worst was upon him, and the evil bite that would cannibalize his nature was about to close upon him, Beathan leaped boldly onto the beast's back stabbing vigorously with a dagger in one hand while clutching wildly with the other to the mane of hair on the creature's head. Beathan's legs had clamped hold of the creature's side, and he was administering strike after strike of his dagger into its shoulders and neck.

The thing screamed in pain, rage and with what Philip, after years of collecting strange and fantastical beasts, had come to understand as fear. It screamed and wailed until the end came and Beathan ruthlessly dug his dagger into its throat and severed the neck all the way to the spine. As if by afterthought, the half-breed jabbed his dagger into one of its eyes, a parting gift for the painful punch from earlier. The fairy gypsy was lively and fun when on your team, but he had a decidedly nasty streak when it came to his enemies. Philip couldn't fault him, however. There were few creatures with less of their humanity left than the Wendigo.

Beathan slid off its back tiredly and the Wendigo crumpled to the ground dead. No birds sang, no crickets chirped; the stillness felt as final as its death. Slowly, ever so slowly, the beast began to shrink. Its hair

The Collector

whitened gradually and then fell off in large clumps. It shriveled in on itself until it was the size of a man. Beathan and Philip watched in silence, relieved the fight was over and that they had both survived unharmed.

Philip glanced up at Beathan when it was over and in confusion, saw that the half-fairy's hair had lightened a shade, and a few wrinkles had appeared where they hadn't been before.

"Is that what happened to the vampires this morning?" Beathan asked, pointing at the dead Wendigo.

Philip nodded yes. "How do you feel, Beathan? You look—" he paused unsure of how to say it tactfully, "—older."

Beathan nodded his head wearily. "I feel older. 'Tis the bonding, the tainted magic from the magician I think." He flashed a grin at Philip. "But I'll let you in on a little secret, I'm not nearly as young as I look. Part o' me charm is the ability to retain youthfulness longer than a normal man. I guess I am only now beginning to look closer to me true age."

Philip smiled wanly. If the fairy wanted to play this off then so be it. "Well, the vampires drained of life much quicker than this, or you for that matter," he added, "Possibly the stronger the creature the slower the process."

Beathan slapped his chest tiredly, but was determined to retain his sunny disposition, "I'm resilient, stronger than I look."

Philip and he mounted their horses and regained their course towards Alayna's house. After the fever pitch of battle, Philip could not immediately bring himself to regain their previous conversation. However, after sufficient time had passed, he felt it was time to continue. Philip decided to ask the fairy to explain his bracelet.

"Why don't we pick up where we left off? What's the significance of the bracelet?"

Beathan rolled his eyes good-naturedly but seemed resigned to the fact that the discussion was inevitable. Philip supposed even a creature as cheerful and open as Beathan had secrets that they preferred remained untold. After all, Philip had kept his own hidden for years. The fairy gave in, and opened his mouth to answer as the steady drumbeat of the horses' hooves signaled their trajectory towards a safe haven. "Well, the bracelet is sort o' like an amplifier o' sorts." He paused to let the information sink in. "That devious old magician had done his homework. I know it because he whisked the thing off me wrist quick as ya' like without wasting a moment's time figuring out which one he wanted."

Philip didn't like the way this sounded. The magician was already building power by harnessing the energy of supernatural creatures, and if you added a magical device to the mix, it was bound to get even worse.

"Why do ya' think I wear this lot?" Beathan shook his arms clattering the bracelets against one another. "It's mainly due to me desire to conceal me most precious item, and now it's gone."

Their conversation spun and turned around the incident, trying to piece information together. Beathan did what he could to describe the magician. From his memory, it was a man with a suit and cane, who looked to be in his sixties. It could describe most of the magicians who Philip had encountered in the last decades. Not for the first time today, Philip wished he had James to ask for advice, or even Mr. Astori, however cold he was at times.

"When it comes to it and we find this degenerate," Philip said, speaking of the magician, "how do you believe we can stop him? Can we just take the bracelet to end the spell or will we have to kill him?"

"He used the bracelet to harness me," Beathan answered, "so the charm bracelet is integral to his ability to carry out whatever evil plot he may have. Taking the bracelet is the most important thing." He shook his head. "However, we'd probably have to kill him t' take the bracelet anyhow, so it's a bit of a moot point." Beathan paused then continued, "Besides, the old devil's not goin' t' stop. I seen the look in his eyes when he took me and there were a rare form o' madness there." He looked intently into Philip's eyes, "The kind o' crazy that can't be stopped without lethal means."

Philip understood. The half-breed was making sure that Philip knew that they had to finish this mission to the end. Of all the missions on which Philip had ever been, this was fast becoming the most urgent and important. It might require a gritty finish, but he committed within himself to follow the course to the end, whatever that end might be. Beathan saw the truth of it in his eyes and grinned his approval in a toothy, wolf-like grin. Philip was relieved that at least for now, the half-

The Collector

breed was on his side. After watching him dispose of that Wendigo, Philip was pretty certain that Beathan had been more merciful with him last night than he had realized.

"The bracelet sort o' adds to and enhances whatever ability ya' happen to be using," Beathan felt obligated to explain further it seemed. "It allowed me to dabble in charms and see success, run faster, move my hands more quickly." Move his hands more quickly; Philip didn't want to think at the moment what type of trickery Beathan had been imposing upon people. It sounded like a powerful device indeed. "For you," the Irish fairy volunteered, "It would probably just add to the strength with which ya' have already been bestowed."

Bad news. A magician could tap into that power and enhance their abilities more than Philip wanted to imagine. He had known quite a few witches who would love to get their hands on that bracelet. He shuddered to imagine the fist of terror that would clamp down upon his heart at all of the evil they could accomplish if they were in possession of the bracelet now. This magician must be no different. Only the blackest of hearts took the lives of others without good reason, such as in self-defense, or in the defense of others. Not all had Philip's integrity however. Hardly anybody did he realized sadly. The earth was full of the greedy, selfish and the downright wicked. Yet there were also the Alaynas of the world as well. He focused his thoughts on her, and surrendered to the hopeful, musings of a man who had nothing left but to wish for the best in a difficult endeavor.

Chapter Six

They rode on in silence for the rest of the evening. It seemed an interminable amount of time from the scene of the fight with the Wendigo before they reached Alayna's house, due to Philip's worry over her wellbeing. However, sure enough they found themselves riding up to her abode while there was still a hint of light in the sky.

Her cottage was a humble residence with only two rooms. It had sleeping quarters, and a larger room, combining kitchen, dining area and a small portion of the room allotted as a sitting area.

He and Beathan approached from the east and the evening sun sank fully behind the hills framing the house as they tied their horses to the trees by the gate. After having dismounted and attended to the business of tying up their horses to a fencepost, they strode warily along the twenty feet of stepping-stones pressed into the ground. The tiny path leading from the gate to the front door cut through a neatly engineered and well-kept garden. The garden was clearly meant more to provide self-sufficiency than beauty, as the rows of produce sprouting one after another attested; however, flowers also lined the edges of the garden and lent a faint fragrance to the air. The garden was obviously created with a woman's touch. Philip loved the way everything to which Alayna put her hand became better and more beautiful because of it. There were not many people of which he could say the same thing.

The two of them stopped before the front door and glanced at one another somewhat apprehensively. The one window into the house revealed a lit lamp, as well as a fireplace flickering and flaming, which cast a merry light across the walls of the cottage. But silence accompanied the crackling of the fire and nobody could be seen through the window. Whether Alayna was there or not was still to be seen. Philip

The Collector

prayed that she was. She had to be, he told himself. He hadn't told anyone about her.

Beathan allowed Philip the honor of placing a hand on the quaint, but functional wooden door and pushing inward upon it. It did not bode well that the latch had not been set allowing them to enter with ease. Alayna was a wise and cautious young woman, living alone just outside the city. She kept her doors locked at night.

It creaked as it opened and revealed a peaceful scene. There was a warm fire crackling, and a weathered, much-loved book, the pages creased and worn with use lying open on the table, as if left only for a moment by the owner. The scent of a meal freshly baked wafted to their senses reminding Philip of just how hungry he was. It had been breakfast since he had last eaten and his belly began to flip-flop and turn in upon itself in a gurgling fashion as it tried to eat its way out of his body. Alayna had always known how to cook a good meal. It smelled like stew, his favorite. Beathan looked at him and smiled in anticipation of the meal at hand.

Philip, however, wasn't so certain that all was well. The door had been unlocked. Something was off.

"Alayna," he called out softly, carefully, "my dear, are you here?" The silence in response to his answer rang louder in his ears than any shout could have. He rushed over to the door to her sleeping quarters, filled with worry for the girl who he realized he had come to love. To hell with his fear and doubt and all this ceaseless caution, all that mattered was finding Alayna and making sure she was safe.

Nothing, the room was empty, the bed unmade. It was his precious Alayna's one area in which she lacked propriety and cleanliness. He couldn't force the normal smile he felt when he saw the disorderly state in which she always allowed her bed to remain. Normally, he would have laughed at how the rest of her home and the surrounding property were ordered to the finest detail, and as clean as a country home could possibly be, but not tonight. The dull ache of fear replaced the hunger in his belly, clamping down on his heart and nerves like never before. He needed to find her.

Even prior to Beathan calling out from the next room that he had found a note left by an anonymous author, Philip could feel the menacing hand of the magician, whom they pursued, orchestrating the events of tonight. The Wendigo slowing them, preventing them from reaching Alayna's house earlier, only to arrive and find her just gone, food still in the pot.

He stepped briskly back into the common room and leaned over the table with Beathan to study the note. Philip resolved within himself to become ice. He shoved the fear and nerves that he normally felt during hunting and collecting aside and became numb with purpose. The only thing that was left for him to do was to solve the mystery and stop the enemy, thereby saving Alayna. He had no doubt in his mind that whoever was behind this was an enemy of the direst kind.

The note was simple. It didn't have many words but the words that were written on the page simultaneously chilled Philip to the bone and set a fire of anger and betrayal raging in his heart. The note read:

"Follow the north fork of the road until you reach the estate. You'll know to which one I refer when you reach it. Do not delay; the girl's life depends on it. A return of the old, a rebirth is upon us. Some secrets are too potent to be kept hidden from those who know us well."

Philip crumpled the letter and threw it into the fire. It flamed up into a quick, furious burn and then turned to ash. It didn't matter; the directions were seared into his brain. Beathan seemed to realize that Philip had understood the note, had deciphered a hidden, personal meaning out of it.

"Would ya' care t' enlighten me as to what manner of revelation that held for ya'?" Beathan asked soberly. The half-breed who Philip had met last night in his attempted Collection had appeared no older than his early twenties. The one that stared at him through the deceptively cheery light of the fire, which had been crafted to hold the bitter cold of winter at bay, now looked to be closer to Philip's own age; a man in his late thirties or possibly early forties.

Philip raged silently inside himself, but kept his voice cool and calm as he answered, it would not do to give in to his emotions at such a crucial moment as this. "Indeed, I shall," he said. "The last phrase there reveals the vile culprit, a man of dear trust to me." Philip seethed. "That he would engineer such a daring and dastardly escapade such as this,

The Collector

resulting in the death of my partner and the abduction of my woman, is the foulest of betrayals."

Beathan read between the lines well. He saw what Philip had to mean by his comment on trust. "So it's an inside job then." His Irish accent pierced the stillness, quietly but surely the sound of a man voicing a truth he didn't want to vocalize but had to speak nonetheless.

Philip nodded and Beathan whistled in distressed wonder. The half-fairy continued, "A member himself. I never thought I'd witness the day when the Guild turned upon its own. Truly, I hold no great love for the Collector's Guild, wanted man that I am. But 'tis also true that I have no desire to see the masses hurt. I have always supported the Guild's work, when done with pure intentions, pertaining t' the collection of those creatures that truly are wicked in heart and in nature."

Beathan laughed as he danced a small jig while speaking the next line of thought. "Well," he amended in addition to the previous statement, "I've always supported the Guild's purposes, except in certain cases, the likes o' which shall remain anonymous." He grinned and bowed, indicating that he was speaking of himself. "Have peace me friend, we'll find her."

His ending words, a consolation of the most general sort, somehow pierced Philip's icy resolve and he found his emotions welling up. It did indeed feel important to have an accomplice in this venture, a partner upon which he could trust. He looked gratefully at Beathan and was surprised to find that in such a short span of time he had found that the half-breed was truly an honorable man, and a friend.

Philip furthered Beathan's understanding of the situation. "The man behind this is a high member of the guild, a senior member," he paused regretfully, "and I must admit he is my personal overseer, not to mention my oldest family friend. Mr. Astori was the man I trusted most after my partner James."

Beathan quirked his mouth and twisted his head, a nonverbal communication of commiseration, then clapped his hand on Philip's shoulder. "We'll catch him," he repeated his earlier platitude, but somehow Philip knew that when Beathan said it he meant it. He took heart and believed. If he lost faith in their abilities to accomplish what was difficult, he feared more than just his love would perish or worse by the end of these results. He felt that he must enlighten his new partner further.

They hurried out the door to the horses and set course for the north fork of the road as they had been instructed. There wasn't time to waste, and no time to plan, but too important a life was at stake for Philip to second guess whether obeying the directions given by the betrayer Mr. Astori was a good plan.

As they rode in the darkness of early night, the stars speckling the sky above them like motionless fireflies in a wood, he told Beathan the added horror of which he suspected Mr. Astori.

"I fear that there is much more afoot here than just murder, abduction, and the loosing of dangerous creatures," he began, and Beathan nodded sagely as if he had suspected the same all along. Philip continued, "Mr. Astori made mention of the old returning, and a rebirth in his note. I greatly fear that he is somehow attempting to initiate all over again the Great Transformation."

Philip stated the last two words resolutely for emphasis, but Beathan did not seem as horrified as he had anticipated. He simply shook his head wryly, as if he had seen it coming and wasn't that afraid of it. Philip was forced to remember that his new partner was as much or more supernatural a being than human. *You are partly non-human also*, a small voice whispered in the back of his mind. He shoved the truth of it aside roughly, leaving it for another time, and focused on the currently one-sided discussion.

"Does that not concern you, friend?" he asked of the fairy.

Beathan waited a moment before answering. The hooves of their horses thudded in the thinly wooded land, and they rode through hills and glades split by a man made contrivance, however convenient, a road. Beathan studied nature around them. He gazed silently at the bright and shining moon, as it mirrored the reflections of the thousands of stars around it one hundred fold, casting a pale but determined light upon the road.

Finally, he spoke, "Is that so bad? Are we so bad?" Beathan placed a hand on his chest near his heart almost subconsciously revealing that the *we* about which he spoke were the myriad of non-human entities alive in the world.

The Collector

"In answer to your first question, yes," Philip responded, "and to the second, no. Of course not."

Beathan squinted at him as the moonlight illuminated Philip's face beside him. Philip recognized that look. It was the look of a person who wished to simply be, to exist in a world free from the fear of being hunted. But nearly all the creatures pursued by the Guild were much worse and more dangerous than the one who rode beside Philip tonight. Philip was certain that the fairy would have ridden into whatever lay ahead no matter the predicament in which he found himself. It was the right thing to do, and Beathan, although he had questionable morals about property rights and tricks, did what was good and true when it counted. It was more than he could say for most humans.

Philip continued to speak. "But not all creatures are as neutral to the conflicts of human and non-human as fairies. Many of the supernatural beings in the world are invariably and despicably evil." Philip waited to go on until he saw the reluctant agreement in his partner's face.

"There are malevolent entities at loose on the earth that are bent on the one sole purpose—the ruin and destruction of mankind. Whether that be en masse or one at a time, their aim of existence is to survive and feed on the lives of others." His disgust at such selfishness and evil rang out in his voice. "The world would be subject to a horror that I fear it could not survive should another Great Transformation be brought upon us."

"I see your point," Beathan answered, "an' I agree. Yet I cannot reconcile the way you tend t' group all me fellow non-humans into one bunch. 'Specially when ya' consider the fact that you yourself belong to the same class o' beings of which you speak."

Philip knew it was true, but he had spent so many years denying his non-human side, only tapping into it when there was no other choice, in the case of a life or death moment or fight. It was hard to come to terms with the reality of his hybrid genetic makeup.

Beathan added, "It is not about choosing sides. It's about living a life that does no harm t' others and living a life that's free." They rode onward at a fast clip and the fairy lifted his hand up into the air, as if feeling something that Philip did not. "Freedom is so much more 'n living your life outside o' a cell with locks an' bars. It's about letting the wind speak t' ya', t' tell ya' where t' go and when t' do it. It's about having the ability t' run when your fear gets the better o' courage, an' having the right to stand an' fight when your conscience tells ya' to." He dropped his hand and, pointing a finger at Philip, emphasizing that now was one of those times.

This was a different side to Beathan than he had experienced in the hours since they had met. Beathan the thief, the runner, the light-hearted trickster and even the warrior Philip could understand and expect. However, the fairy as philosopher seemed out of place, or Philip realized at least out of the normal.

Beathan smiled at Philip as if reading his mind. "Not what ya' expected of the half-gypsy pickpocket, hey?" He threw back his head and laughed as if it were the funniest thing he had said. His hair trailed behind him in a mane, blowing freely in the wind as they raced onwards. The fairy dropped the reins, stretched his arms out to his sides and tilted his head backwards, letting his body become one with the movements of the horse.

They galloped and Philip stared at his reckless partner. Yet in doing so, the Irish fairy couldn't help but symbolize perfectly the point he had just been making. They headed into who knew what. They might possibly experience a moment of heroism, but this venture was much more likely to result in their deaths. In the face of that, the fairy exemplified the freedom to choose about which he had been speaking. Whether death or life awaited them, the half-breed had chosen to face it willingly. No one, nor any thing, had forced him to ride this moonlit road with Philip tonight.

The dawning of something new began inside of Philip. No longer could he reconcile what the Guild did. Of course, the majority of those beings he Collected were deserving of it, but there were often those like Beathan, half-breeds or full-born of a more harmless race. They were pegged as dangerous or violent, or simply too downright mischievous. They were added to the list of convicts that the Guild pursued, and when captured locked away with the worst of them never to be seen or heard from again. Philip wondered how many of those he had put behind bars or deep within the St. Thomas's vault-like, below-ground cells without realizing it. The thought pained him no end.

The Collector

The fairy relaxed back into a normal, fluid, riding stance and glanced at Philip from the corner of a narrowed eye. He smiled again, and this was yet another new smile, a smile conveying that he saw his words were having a genuine impact on the way Philip was thinking. He said nothing and Philip was glad. He wasn't sure he wanted the moment interrupted. Philip's wish for a moment of reprieve wasn't granted for long however, as a few short seconds later they passed under an overhanging tree and all hell broke loose.

As they rode under the branches, four figures dressed in dark clothing dropped lithely from the trees onto him and Beathan. Clobbered out of their saddles they landed in the dust of the road, panting and frantically trying to gain a sense of what was happening. Daggers were out in both of Beathan's quick hands and he twirled them menacingly, slicing at the two figures that surrounded him, as they darted in at him from opposite sides of his body. Their enemies had split their band into two groups of two to keep Philip and his new partner at a disadvantage.

Philip's own reactions yielded him a silver dagger from his belt and a wooden stake from his boot, as he shot to his own feet a hair slower than his quicksilver, fairy partner. It was good that Philip let his instincts guide his hands as he rose because sure enough, the faces illuminated by the moonlight were not human, belonging to a dark pair of figures circling him with wicked grins on their faces. A vampire, its pallid, sunken face giving way to a wide mouth framed by fangs on either side, came at him from his left and he fended it off desperately yet with his usual manner of experience. The other side of his body was set upon by a werewolf, its red eyes shrieking the madness that lay within its head. Philip looked up and sure enough, the moon was full. On a full moon, all sanity and reason left a werewolf. This would almost certainly be his more dangerous of opponents. It was a good thing he had brought his silver dagger. Philip used it liberally, slicing fur, and cleaving the flesh off the arms of the werewolf as it lunged in again and again mindlessly ignoring the wounds Philip inflicted.

He was hard pressed to fight his own battle let alone keep an eye on whether Beathan was faring any better. Philip's two opponents, thankfully, had not had much experience working together because there was no coordination in their attacks, which was probably what allowed him to survive those first few moments of the ambush.

Philip's calm focus from earlier took over and he calculated his moves with a chilly detachment. He turned his attack gradually towards the werewolf, lopping off a few of its clawed fingers as it flailed its body at him in a powerful but disorganized assault. His attention on the wolf was just enough to lure the vampire in at his back, as he had planned, and with some careful foot work, he lunged at the werewolf, then pivoted, already swinging his other hand up and around in a powerful, might infused strike, burying the stake into the surprised vampire's heart.

It had been attempting to take him unawares, and instead scrabbled at the death planted in its chest uselessly, with its suddenly weak hands, before toppling to the ground and withering up like the two vampires earlier that morning. It made sense, and yet it did not. The vampire withered, and as Philip studied his remaining opponent he saw that the same was happening, albeit much more slowly, to the werewolf. To Philip, this signified that they must both have been bonded and sent by the magician. It also explained the fact that a vampire and werewolf, two typically adverse creatures, were abandoning their usual animosity and working in unison. However, Philip was still experiencing confusion as to why the magician would have summoned them in his note and then sent these minions to kill them. That part made no sense.

As the werewolf continued its reckless and haphazard assaults, Philip was able to catch a glimpse of his partner's own battle. Beathan whirled in his out-of-date clothing, coat tails and knives swirling equally in the moonlight. He hadn't managed to dispose of either of his attackers as Philip had, but he was holding his own, and inflicting wounds that were bound to take their toll.

Philip focused his attention back upon the werewolf slobbering on itself, in an insane excitement to get its jaws on him. He decided it was high time to deal with this beast, what was once a *man* he reminded himself automatically, and go to the aid of his partner.

Philip eyed the werewolf and closed the ground between them warily. There was no pomp or flair to the way Philip fought, no tossing of knives back and forth between hands the way street fighters were known to do to impress the crowds of onlookers they often drew in a

The Collector

city. No, this was the wild. This was about survival, and this was what Philip was good at, for what he had trained, for what he was built.

Methodically, he wore the creature down, dodging in to slash and cut, then bounding back out of range of the claws and teeth. He kept moving, circling it, and finally after feinting left and then cutting right he pulled another knife, a normal one from his belt and threw it accurately at the beast's chest, then followed his knife throw with his more deadly silver dagger. The knife he threw stuck into the right side of the werewolf's chest, just above its ribs, causing it to stagger back slightly from the impact. Philip was then upon it and was too close for the reach of the werewolf's wildly swinging, clawed hands. It was a quick finish. The thing growled and grasped at Philip as best it could, but Philip's silver dagger made mincemeat of its stomach, spilling entrails onto the ground like a melon burst open after falling off a cart.

The beast moaned and then collapsed, allowing Philip to turn to Beathan's aid. The fairy seemed to have withered slightly as well, to be moving just a little bit more slowly. Philip glanced back to check his fallen victim to be sure of its death and saw its hair going white and its wolfish blend of muzzle and man's face shrinking slowing but surely.

He turned back to the fight and saw that Beathan's two foes were both vampires, and he pulled another stake from his other boot and threw it with all of his might at the closer of the two vampires. It flew true, and hit the back of one's skull with crushing impact, penetrating until the point stuck out the eye socket on the other side. It twitched as it crumpled to the earth. The heart wasn't the only vulnerable spot on a vampire. A brain worked just as well. The other vampire saw its last ally go down and set upon Beathan in a crazed frenzy, something about its actions suggesting more than the normal vampiric aggression—a spell of some kind perhaps. But with only one vampire remaining, Beathan made quick work of it and before long it was dead, lying face down in the dirt of the road with the others. It had all happened in what couldn't have been more than a few minutes, but Philip couldn't help but feel enraged at the wasted minutes, the time spent dealing with these brutes instead of pursuing his beautiful Alayna.

"You sure you still want to come along?" Philip questioned somewhat wryly as he panted with his hands resting on his knees. The fairy had a few scratches and a bite mark on his neck, but seemed to be holding up well enough for all he had been through in the last twenty-four hours.

The fairy grinned his usual grin, although this time it came from the face of a man, just slightly older than what Philip looked to be. The spell he was under was taking its effect as he used his powers and abilities to defend himself. "Ya' go on an' worry 'bout yourself now, laddy," he laughed, "I can take care meself just fine." He punctuated his sentence with a last kick at the nearest body and they both laughed together then, somehow finding comedy in the midst of what had to be almost the worst day imaginable for them both.

The horses were gone, fled in the attack, so they ran lightly up the road, continuing in the direction they had been instructed. North for not too much longer and they reached the mansion spoken of in the note left on Alayna's table. It was a grand, old place, the kind of building that must once have been filled with pride and love by its owners, but now fallen into great disregard as it had been abandoned. Torches lit the path leading up to the front door, showing spider webs and grime filling the windows. It was three stories or more, but only the bottom floor had light pouring out of the windows, so Philip was fairly certain that whoever was holding Alayna was there.

He turned to his partner, "Beathan," he whispered, "Astori only knows that I am coming. I'll go in the front door alone, draw his attention and you can find another way in and surprise him. It's the best plan," he answered in response to the questioning look he was receiving from the fairy.

"Do ya' think it wise to separate?" the fairy asked. "I know this man's strength perhaps better than you after being captured. He's not the sort to face alone."

"I'll draw his attention," he responded, "You find a way to get the bracelet and curtail his increasing power."

Philip understood the fairy's concern, it was valid no doubt, but surprise was the only advantage they might possess. If what they had seen was true, each beast they had killed had only added to the magician's power, let alone what had happened with the rest of the escaped convicts. He convinced Beathan of this, and so it was that he

The Collector

approached the steps to the mansion and climbed them alone as the fairy circled around to the side of the building.

As he reached the door, it swung open of its own accord, and a voice reverberated from the rotting wood of the door frame and the dirty floor boards in front of Philip, "Come in, Philip."

The voice of the man Philip had admired for so long before now sounded hollow and ugly. It had always been cold, but Philip's admiration for the man had added a noble quality to it that was forever gone now, leaving it sounding harsh, the wickedness of its intentions open to his perception. It also sounded deeper, but at the same time fuller, a younger voice, however evil it was. It was hard to come to terms with the change.

The body-less voice echoed out again, "I know you hate me at this moment Philip, but perhaps that will change as you hear me out." Philip did not know the extent of Astori's powers as a magician, but they seemed to somehow entail a form of mind reading, however, it was possible that he was just very good at guessing.

Philip followed the sound of the voice into the bowels of the house, it was a maze of dimly lit hallways enshrouded with webs, and rooms stripped of everything but the barest of necessities. Torches were placed in sconces on the walls, casting a dull, flickering light across the floor and walls.

The way inward did not take as long as he anticipated due to how large the estate appeared from the exterior. As he arrived at what he supposed to be the final door before encountering Astori, he paused. He hoped Beathan would be able to find his own way in separately and secretly through the maze of rooms.

Once again the door creaked inward, opening, just as he raised his hand to touch it. This time no voice accompanied it. Instead, there was an eerie silence, what Philip equated to the calm before the storm, or even more aptly put, the eye of the storm, where a moment of stillness and silence was a brief reprieve from the chaos and mayhem preceding and following it.

Philip walked into the room and looked around. It was a spacious room, open to a balcony surrounding it from the second floor like a completely enclosed interior courtyard. A chair with his beloved Alayna in it sat in the middle of the room. She was chained to it and her head leaned limply against the side. He knew she wasn't dead because otherwise why chain her? But the fear he felt that she might be harmed threatened to consume him. A figure stepped out of the shadows, walking theatrically with a cane it no longer needed. The man he stared at in the dim light of the room was more youthful than he would have imagined. Whereas Beathan had aged considerably in the last twenty-four hours, the reverse was true for Astori. He looked to be a few years younger than Philip now, possibly in his late thirties.

The man who had regressed to his prime smiled icily at Philip, "Incredible isn't it? What one can do with unlimited power?" The whites of his teeth bore no charm or warmth; they were simply a tool of a man used to getting his way with persuasive words.

Philip stared at him keeping his silence. He felt nothing but hate for the man, but as long as Astori stood next to Alayna, he was reluctant to anger the man needlessly. Astori strutted until he stopped within a few feet from Alayna, and Philip stayed where he was near the entrance of the room.

"Well, what do you think?" Astori finally broke the silence with his vain question, motioning to the body he now possessed that was forty years younger than it should have been. Again, Philip stayed silent.

"Well?" The evil magician now seemed impatient for a response.

Philip was worried he would now grow angry without a response so he resolved to answer him. This was a terrible situation, and as much as he wished to lie and protect Alayna, Astori knew him well enough to see through whatever untruth he told. The truth would serve him best now.

"You disgust me," he answered plainly, calmly.

Astori threw back his head and laughed, clapping his hands together, making a sound that echoed in the empty room.

"Still pure, even to the end, my boy." Astori quirked an eyebrow. "Or I suppose I should call you Philip now that our ages are not so discrepant."

Philip took a slow, cautious step toward the center of the room before responding. "Astori, sir," he filled the honorary title with as much sarcasm and disdain as he could, "leave Alayna out of this. You don't need her. This has nothing to do with her."

The Collector

"And what do you know of whether this has anything to do with her?" Astori smirked in answer.

"I know that you have been changing people into creatures, and I suspect you are trying to elicit another Great Transformation," Philip said matter-of-factly, trying hard not to look at the magician's wrist with the bracelet. He couldn't afford to tip off Astori to the fact that he knew of the amplifier. Where was Beathan?

Astori seemed pleased to discuss his devious plan. Villains always seemed to need somebody with whom they could revel in what they perceived to be the genius of their accomplishments. Apparently, Astori had no fear of Philip and was willing to share his plans. So be it. Philip was used to being underestimated, and the more he learned of Astori's plan the better. Philip kept him talking.

"Indeed, Philip that is the very thing I desire. Another widespread mania will sweep the continent, if not the globe, and I'll be the one to benefit." He was extremely pleased with himself. It was an ugly sentiment, the way Philip imagined a fat, old spider would look as it watched its helpless prey, wrapped up tightly and waiting for the blood to be siphoned from its still kicking body.

"Why do you need Alayna?" Philip held his breath as he waited for the answer.

"I need a catalyst, a human focal point, for my work here tonight," Astori commented idly, picking and cleaning a fingernail, as if the conversation was all of a sudden the most boring thing in the world. "I would imagine you have pieced together some of the puzzle by now," Astori said. "I venture to guess that some idea must have begun to form in your mind after surviving the encounter with that young vampire and his friend I sent to you this morning." He flourished toward the dirty quarters and stated in mock humility, "I can transform one person at a time into a being of supernatural ability, but to do so on a widespread level requires a subject to be the focal point of my magic. A catalyst," he concluded where he had begun, idly fingering something beneath his coat sleeve. He was still dressed like a gentleman in a coat, and pants, and hat, only now he had opted for a dashing suit of modern standards rather than the slightly worn one in which Philip was accustomed to seeing him as part of his disguise.

"Why send the flowers or the note then?" Philip questioned further.

Astori seemed close to declining to answer then seemed to shake his head as if it mattered little whether or not he disclosed more information to Philip. "After you survived the vampires this morning, I needed to keep you occupied. There is a whole shipload full of our," he smiled and looked for the best word, "friends, raging rampant across the city, and I grow stronger with every passing act of violence they commit." He closed his hands into fists and squeezed as if he could literally feel the strength being added to him as they used their supernatural abilities.

Philip took another step closer, "I see," he said carefully. "And Alayna? Why involve her? You don't need her. Was it out of some evil spite?" He clenched his teeth in anger at the thought.

Astori threw back his head and laughed. "Spite! Ha! As if you were important enough to me to involve her for that reason. No, my dear Philip, she was simply a convenient subject to use for the catalyst, right on the way here."

"So you didn't bring her here to lure me?" Philip asked, trying to make sense of things, and hoping to keep the man preoccupied with the sound of his own voice, until Beathan arrived. Where was Beathan?

Astori waved a hand dismissively. "I knew you'd follow, but I sent out the quartet of my little minions to apprehend you earlier. Apparently they failed." The magician opened his hand and a puff of smoke preceded a ball of flame that he began throwing back and forth casually between his hands, as if their failure was of no real importance.

The magician continued to speak and Philip allowed him to do so unhindered. The longer he spoke the more chance Philip had of receiving aid from Beathan. "Oh, I'll admit that my slight fondness for your parents, and my small part to play in who you are today," he raised his eyebrows knowingly at Philip signifying the answer to the question Philip had asked him that morning, "made me reluctant to allow your outright death. All day I've given you a way out if you should prove resourceful enough."

It was true, Philip recognized, no situation that he had faced today had been beyond his ability to overcome. They had all tested him, but not beyond the limits of his strength and will.

The Collector

Astori went on, "My earlier endeavors to ignite another Transformation through a catalyst fell short." Philip assumed he was speaking of the boy vampire, but he would not be surprised to learn that there had been others prior to that. "No matter," Astori continued, "the creatures out there wreaking havoc as we speak, are strengthening me through the bond, enough so that my success is certain this time. I can feel it." Astori breathed deep as if sensing a newfound power within himself. "Your little gal over there was my way of keeping you busy, and ensuring that you wouldn't go around righting my wrongs so to speak, until it was too late to matter." The magician lifted a lock of hair from her unconscious head, "Besides, she is a fair one. Not half bad to look at. I could have chosen a far worse catalyst for my little experiment." He ended his statement with a self-deprecating title of what would have monumental consequences for the world if he succeeded. Experiment? Warfare would be a better description.

"I can't let you do it," Philip said calmly, "I can't let you hurt her."

With that Philip threw himself across the remaining space between them. He hurtled painfully into an invisible brick wall as he saw the magician lift his hands in front of him conjuring up some dark spell. Then another spell lifted Philip up off of the ground and with a throwing motion of his hand Astori's magic flung him into the wall on the other side of the room.

Philip shook his head dazedly as he struggled to clear the pain from his head. He managed to make it to his knees before he felt a vice-like invisible hand gripping his throat and forcing him to stay where he was.

Again Astori laughed scornfully; he seemed to be doing a lot of that tonight.

"You? Stop me?" As if to punctuate such a ridiculous question he used his magic to shake Philip like a rag doll until he nearly lost consciousness. "You are powerless against me." He shook his wrist up in the air and a charm bracelet, obviously the one he must have taken from the half-breed, clattered around his wrist. "I have a special prize at my disposal."

He didn't realize Philip knew what he was talking about and he didn't explain further. At the ruckus, Alayna awoke from her slumber. Or from whatever induced unconsciousness had been forced upon her.

"Philip," she murmured groggily, and then as she came to with more force, "Philip!"

The terror in her voice was too much for him to bear. He thrashed and cursed as he struggled to free himself from the unyielding grip that held him on his knees.

"Ahh, our test subject has awakened," Astori said in a velvet voice. He maintained whatever magic imprisoned Philip and strutted over to Alayna. Her green eyes were beautiful, framed by her strawberry gold hair. Normally they were filled with life and joy, but tonight they were clouded with confusion and terror. She had known of Philip's reality and his work. He had not kept that from her. However, this was her first time experiencing anything out of the normal, everyday existence of a human.

"If you harm her I'll kill you," Philip vowed, an empty oath in his present circumstances, but imbued with as much wrath as he could muster. An invisible fist landed a massive blow to his head.

Astori sneered at him. "You'll do as you're told or it will go worse for her. Besides, I suppose I am doing you a favor after all. Now, she'll truly be like you."

Philip stared at him uncomprehendingly and Alayna turned her head back and forth from Philip to Astori in confusion.

"Oh, I see," Astori commented slyly, taking delight in the secret he held, "you haven't told her. How furtive of you—downright despicable."

This would not have been the setting he would have chosen to tell Alayna about the anomaly of his genetics, his strength, and the way he had healed as a child. But it appeared that Astori wasn't quite ready to divulge his information and end the game of cat and mouse that he played with Philip's emotions. Instead of speaking further, the magician put one hand on the amplifier he wore at his wrist and then placed the other hand to Alayna's forehead. He began muttering incantations too low for Philip to hear, but Alayna began to thrash and writhe in her chains, unable to escape what was happening. A soft light began to spread, lightly luminescent across the room and out the doors, through the walls. It spread and Philip had no doubt that it was the Great Transformation all over again. The first transformation may not have come by the hands of a man, but this one was. Judging by how fast the luminescence had spread at first, and the moments that had now elapsed,

The Collector

it must now have reached nearly one hundred feet outside the mansion, Philip speculated, and all the while he could do nothing.

At that moment a shape leapt from the balcony above him straight down to the floor beside Astori. In a swift movement, Beathan unsheathed a dagger and with a powerful swipe of his hand cut clean through the arm with the hand placed on Alayna's head. The hand fell to the ground and blood spattered across Alayna's beautiful face.

Astori screamed in pain and rage and stared dumbfounded at the stump of a hand that now stared back at him. However, he immediately recovered from his shock because as Beathan reached down and grasped the charm bracelet that belonged to him, Astori summoned whatever dark arts there were at his disposal and delivered such a blow of magic to the fairy that he flew across the room and lay in a stunned pile against the wall. Beathan still clutched the bracelet.

Astori sneered at Philip as he tried to rise again and the invisible hand that held Philip down turned into a hand with claws that dug painfully into his body. Blood ran down Philip's back and chest as a vicious claw inflicted what revenge it could upon him. Philip gritted his teeth in pain and it was all he could do to not black out from the sheer agony of what felt like a handful of knives stabbing into his body.

"Fools!" Astori panted as he created a ball of flame in his good hand and cauterized his wound with another grunt of pain. "I'm still too strong for you, even without the bracelet. I have harnessed the power of all those creatures, and their might saps from them and feeds me." He nodded towards Alayna. "I only needed to draw upon the magnifying power of the bracelet to initiate the enchantment I cast on Alayna, and that is now spreading even as we speak. There's nothing you can do!" he remarked arrogantly. "The spell is bound to me, not the bracelet." He slammed Philip to the ground as if to prove his point.

Beathan still lay motionless against the wall, and Astori made no move to reacquire the bracelet. Perhaps it was true that he did not need it. That did not bode well for the three of them. And then, as if to add to the problems, Alayna began to slowly change. As Philip first saw her shift it was only the slightest of touches around her face. He feared she was withering just like the bonded creatures had. But it was not so. Astori smirked evilly as he noticed the same thing Philip had. They watched the changes take place in silence. Alayna thrashed, seeming to realize something was happening to her, and that she was the subject of their focus.

Her face thinned ever so slightly and her features lengthened just a bit. It only added to her beauty, lending her an exotic look. Her hair hanging loosely revealed an ear to them, and its smoothly rounded top grew into a point, beautifully and elegantly tipped. Even her voice changed into a more musical, melodious lilt as she asked Philip what was happening. He knew what was happening. The Great Transformation had been reinitiated magically, and she was the first subject, she was the catalyst.

Alayna stared at Philip, silently beseeching him to do something. It was too much. He could give in to despair no longer. There had to be a way out of this predicament. Suddenly he knew what he had to do.

For so long Philip had denied every part of himself that he deemed not normal or inhuman. His strength was the main point of inhumanity of which he had been confronted, and for so long he had succumbed to using it only in the direst of circumstances. Even in those situations he had felt dirty, a cheat, unclean, as he used non-human ability to capture and hold those similarly non-human, regardless of whether they deserved it or not. For too long he had ignored the truth, the reality of what he was. It was time to surrender.

Alayna was changing, had changed for all he could tell, and the world was about to be transformed as well, probably the majority for ill if he couldn't do something. What was the use of clinging to the façade of his complete humanity? The blood transfusion that had occurred years ago during his sickly childhood had assimilated the troll's genetics into his own to some degree. There had to be more there than just strength. He had been healed of sickness supernaturally as a child upon the initial blood transfusion, which told him that the healing gift of the troll's blood had been assimilated into his own body. However, never since then had he experienced healing properties other than that of a normal human being. Not in all his fights and scuffles over the years had his body healed the way it had when he was a boy. Why was that? The only idea that came to Philip was that somehow, along the way, his mind or some other deeper part of his being that controlled his body must have masked

The Collector

some of the characteristics, other than the strength, in a subconscious effort to cling to normality. His ability to heal quicker than normal must have been masked along with those, explaining why he had not experienced it during the intervening years from then until now. However, now Philip knew, and he finally accepted the fact that he was not fully human. It was time to relinquish his claim on humanity and accept the true reality that awaited within him. He embraced his whole self for what he truly was, a half-breed like Beathan, and he let free that part of him that was wild to run its course.

He bent his head and closed his eyes. It was as if he stared within himself. He saw the blood pumping through his veins, the heart beating in his chest. He saw the muscles contracting and straining as they strove to free themselves from Astori's magical grasp. He surrendered to it all, the pounding, thudding of his heart and blood filling his ears and mind. He surrendered and searched, looking within himself for the seed of magic, the supernatural seed that lay inside of him along with his strength. Finally he found it. Deep in the recesses of his mind it bloomed. It was as if he saw a gemstone of precious value, blue and uncut, sitting in his unconscious. He focused on it, and it grew to swallow his focus until the gemstone shattered sending sharp pieces of the jewel searing through his consciousness like so many shards of ice spraying as an icicle falls to the ground. The pain was good the way it felt to get in touch with a friend you hadn't seen in a long time. There was joy at rediscovery, but pain and sorrow of time lost. It was just so that he felt now.

Philip opened his eyes and stared at Astori a new man. He tightened his muscles once more and felt the magic flex this time as he strained.

Astori smiled knowingly at him, and said, "So, you have finally surrendered to it. Good, it will be more of a contest now. It took me some time myself to surrender completely. I am glad that you have finally done so. I would have hated to have to kill you without it. That would have been like butchering an unarmed man."

Philip knew that trolls were almost impervious to magic and decided that now was as good a time as any to test out the limits of what had just happened. He strained physically, but this time he strained mentally, tapping into the reservoir of strength that he now knew he possessed in the center of his being, the part of him that accepted his human self in conjunction with his nonhuman self as well.

This time the magic bonds holding him down imposed by Astori flexed and broke, sending the ex-Guild member flying backward, as if something physical had recoiled in his face. Philip bounded to his feet lithely, feeling his usual strength coupled with other traits, new things within himself that had been masked and hidden, subjugated for his whole life by his desire to live as a normal human in a regular existence. There was quickness, cunning, and a troll's all-consuming desire to be in the wild, the mountains, and forests of the north. There was love of the chase and the hunt and the fight, bubbling below the surface like never before. Usually, he avoided, even feared confrontation only doing so when necessary as part of his job, but he could feel himself looking forward to the clash that lay ahead with his old mentor Astori.

Most of all, he felt the imperviousness to magic that he possessed, the ability that would aid him most in this struggle with the magician. He advanced slowly. He knew he looked the same in appearance, but he felt different and Astori sensed it.

"So," the ex-Guild member said drawing out the syllable in thought before repeating the word. "So, you and I are now the same, no longer human." He blinked owlishly at Philip and stated, "I have accepted it long before you though. The advantage is mine." And he rushed Philip initiating the fight.

He flung spells at Philip as he ran, but the part of Philip that was tapping into his supernatural genes brushed them aside as one would flies. Astori snarled as they clattered together, Philip the man of super-human might, against the one handed magician whose magic wouldn't work for him in this fight. However, Philip was not one to underestimate his opponents, and it was good he did not, because it appeared that whatever bond the magician had created with the creatures when he harnessed them had aided him in more ways than could be seen. The spell had given Astori powers beyond that of a magician.

"Your evil magic, your bonding of those non-human entities, has done much more for you physically than just restore your youth," Philip snarled. "How did you manage it?"

The Collector

Astori grinned with a rictus of a smile as they grappled together, upright in front of the miniature prison on which Alayna sat. "Nasty, but neat little trick," Astori answered, "one of the first I picked up although rarely used for its obvious giveaways. I was in Egypt during the Great Transformation and my own shift took on the characteristics of local myths. Their magicians are intricately involved with mummification, so naturally one of the first spells that I acquired happened to be a sort of linked, slow mummification, which transferred the powers of the one that was mummified to me, the one in control as they utilized their gifts."

They were locked close. "Why?" Philip grunted.

"Why? Why not?" Astori practically yelled in apparent fury. "I was changed during the Great Transformation, had to hide who I was in fear of being pursued and locked away." Astori snarled, "I've watched for years as the humans," he said the word with such scorn it hardly sounded like the man Philip had once known, "waste their pitiful lives away, oblivious to reality, and unaware of the cost and sacrifice we Guild members pay to keep them in their safe little cocoons."

His eyes met Philip's and for a moment Philip saw the real man behind this madness, the man that was hurt and frustrated and angry at the world and at the Guild for the way things were. "Your parents were my friends, good loyal Collectors, and they paid for it with their lives. What did they get? Respect? Honor? No, they got a shallow grave and a life with their son cut short." Philip understood the pain, he had felt it more than once himself, but it did not justify this.

He told Astori exactly that. "You cannot take justice into your own hands. Who are you to inflict the Great Transformation upon the world once more?"

The insanity returned to the magician's eyes, and all humanity was gone again. "Why can't I? I'll show the world what life is really like. I'll give them what they deserve, and in the process I'll grow more powerful than anyone as I harness more and more beings." Spittle formed at the corners of the magician's mouth as he practically frothed at the idea of all that power and youth.

Philip had heard enough. He broke their deadlock with his powerful arms and swung his fist in a massive blow, connecting with Astori's now young, face. The magician fell to the ground, but then leapt quickly to

97

his feet more agilely than Philip expected to deliver his own rain of blows as Philip continued to press his own advantage. The fight raged on. Fists struck and nails ripped at each other's faces. Astori used his stub of a hand as effectively as the good one. It was a club instead of a fist.

Not long ago Philip would have been nearly paralyzed with nerves, his resolve to his job with the Guild and devotion to his parents, the only things making him an effective fighter. Of course, after he had met Alayna his love for her drove him onward as well, as it did this day. However, that had all changed a few moments ago. His ability, or capacity perhaps, to stand up for what he believed, and fight when it was needed, had been enhanced. He now embraced his whole self and that had set the wild part of him free. He found himself relishing the battle, the clashing of hands and bodies.

They traded punches and Astori's eye blackened up and became swollen as Philip delivered a smashing over head strike, but the magician's snakelike reflexes allowed him to fight back, landing a shot to Philip's mouth, stunning him somewhat and knocking a tooth out and loosening several others.

Philip recovered, and feeling enraged, fastened his teeth into his opponent's shoulder tearing a piece of flesh out and spitting it on the ground. Blood ran freely from his mouth now, both his own and his enemy's, as they grappled together. In a moment of clarity Philip freed his hand and clasped one of the last knives he had in his belt. He ripped it free and jammed it upwards in one fluid movement into the upper abdomen of Astori.

The man went still in Philip's arms, then jerked once, then again and coughed up blood that ran from his mouth and down Philip's back as Philip held him closely making sure the knife stayed lodged in place, deep within his enemy's vital organs. The magician struggled feebly for a few moments then slumped into death and hung limply in Philip's grasp. He let the dastardly magician fall to the ancient wooden floor and then severed the head from the body in a rough, hewing motion. It never hurt to be certain with non-human beings. Some of them weren't as dead as you always thought; however, none that Philip had encountered could survive a beheading.

The Collector

He panted for a moment, and then forced the wildness that he had set free within himself back down, compartmentalizing it for the time being until he felt his composure and the human side of him return. Philip tore the blood-sodden shirt from his back, as he all of a sudden felt unable to bear that much of another's blood touching his skin. His human side was revolted at the thought of how he had fought—the ferociousness, the wildness with which he had relished the battle. Yet he was a half-breed, truly and self-accepted now, and that non-human part of him knew that it had been necessary to prevail.

He threw the shirt to the ground and his bare, lean, yet muscled chest took ragged breaths as he stared at Alayna. She looked at him as if she had never seen him before. Yet it was not a bad look, it was the look of someone who realized they had been helpless and saved by another.

He walked over and ripped the chains off her with his powerful hands and arms. He had no key and needed none. She leapt to her feet and threw her arms around his neck hugging him desperately. Then her mouth was on his, hot and warm with passion and relief. They continued to kiss until a voice cleared its throat behind them.

Beathan had awakened and was staring at them feigning an innocent expression. "I have me family heirloom again." He wobbled his wrist accordingly with the charm bracelet now reattached, "and it looks like the threat is finished." He eyed the decapitated body on the ground with eyebrows raised.

Philip was composed enough to feel a little bit foolish for having ripped the head off with only a small knife and his hands, but what was done was done and it ensured that Astori wasn't coming back. He clasped Beathan's outstretched hand, keeping one hand wrapped tightly, protectively around his love's waist.

"I can't thank you enough for your aid, Beathan." He stared intently into the half-breed's eyes. "You're a good man."

"Man?" Beathan asked quizzically with a chuckle.

Philip shook his head wryly. "Well, whatever you call yourself, you've done the world, and the Guild, a great service."

Beathan thoughtfully cocked his head sideways and looked at Philip and Alayna meaningfully before answering. "The Guild, eh? Wasn't sure ya'd still be occupying your time doing their bidding." He smiled then, loosening the tension of the statement. "Well, whatever ya' choose t' do, you'll remain a good friend t' me, and one o' the bravest men I know."

Philip inclined his head in thanks at the compliment. "What will you do, Beathan? Where will you go?" He watched the fairy closely, their partnership had been necessary, beneficial, but above all it had been a lifesaving force in the greatest time of need in his life. He wanted to hear the fairy say that he would not be returning to a life of mischief and deceit. Yet Philip now knew what it felt like to surrender to some of the baser instincts of his nature. He understood now how difficult and unsatisfying it could be for some of the non-human beings to try and deny parts of their nature. After all, he had done it for over thirty years and he could now feel the inner peace and emotional release given to him by accepting himself for who he was.

Beathan grinned wildly, his mane of scraggly hair hanging limply on the sides of his face. His aging hadn't regressed but the middle age that he now wore because of the magician's power seemed to fit him perfectly. His appearance painted the picture of a free man who had lived a life of joy without a hook or chain to hold him back. The wrinkles at his eyes could be attributed to the many smiles that he had grinned.

The half-breed seemed to pick up what Philip was thinking and he avoided a set answer. "Suspect I'll return back home t' me isle. I miss the green and mist and dew. Not t' mention, I miss me fairy kin. There are not enough of us on this fair shore. Well, not yet," he glanced meaningfully at Alayna. So he knew. Of course he did, how could he not, he probably felt the shift in her the way Philip did.

Philip nodded sagely. They shook hands again. "You have a friend in me. I owe you my life and much more." Beathan knew he meant Alayna.

"And I you," Beathan commented then in a whisk of movement almost too fast to catch with the naked eye he was gone. With Astori's death the bond was broken and he was free to use his abilities without consequences. His movement was so quick it was like a dash of light.

Alayna giggled slightly in her special way. "I think I like him," she said, her green eyes looking up at Philip from the midst of a smiling face.

The Collector

Philip smiled back. "You should. Without him I would never have been able to stop Astori. I know that I certainly like him and I'll miss him greatly."

Alayna's hand holding his was a comfort at having to watch a friend disappear so quickly after he had been made. It was the fairy's way, they rarely stayed put long, not to mention the gypsy way as well. Philip supposed that he was lucky to have retained his fellow half-breed's focus for so long, nearly a full day.

"I am so glad that you're safe, Alayna," Philip whispered into her ear that was hidden by her silken hair. "I don't know what I would have done if I had lost you." He punctuated the sentence with a kiss to the side of her head.

"Philip," Alayna said in a small voice, not daring to look up at him for some reason. "I'm," she paused in fear, "different now. Are you sure you still want me? All that I am now," she touched her pointed ears, and thin, pale, gorgeous features. Her body was light but strong now, and she finally got the courage to gaze up at him.

She asked again, "How can you accept me now? You have told me how you have dedicated your life and spilt your blood to protect the world from, well, me and my," she paused again, "kind." She trailed off as she struggled to convey the new concept that was her life.

Philip sighed. They may have prevented another Great Transformation, but it was clear to both of them that at least one person had been changed and affected by Astori's enchantment before his death cut it short.

He whispered down at her, "Not you, never from you. I've protected the world from those with whom your love, beauty and purity could never associate. This had to be stopped. You were lucky, my love." He looked at her with a serious gaze. "If this magic had spread, not all people would have been transformed into a being from a race that has the potential to be benevolent, such as yours. Some would have become bloodthirsty, rage-crazed, beasts; monsters in truth."

Alayna nodded her understanding and nuzzled closer to him, relieved at his response that he still wanted her, that there was nothing that could dim his desire for her.

"Do you understand what has happened to you?" he questioned her carefully.

She nodded. "I understand yes, but not the why or the how."

Philip lifted one corner of his mouth in what could only be called a wistful or regretful smile. "Nor I, my love," he responded, "nor I." He looked at Alayna carefully and brushed a stray hair from her face. "How do you know what happened to you during the change?"

She struggled for a moment to come up with a good response, he could tell. Finally she formulated her thoughts well enough to put them into words. "It's like a thousand years of history and memory has been shoved into my brain." She grimaced, but seemed to smile at the same time. "It's hurts, but in a good way, as if I am stretching muscles I haven't used before." She looked at him, "Does that make sense."

"Yes," he answered, and it did. He had heard that some of the beings that inhabited the world had a sort of gestalt consciousness, a oneness of entity that superseded their singular lives. It did not negate their individuality, rather it enhanced it as it allowed them to be consciously aware of their roots, their past, and the origins of their species. Although he doubted many had ever been transformed into being as Alayna had. He had never heard of it happening before. The *Alderfolk,* as those who were now her people were called here in America or the *Alfur* as they were known in Iceland, or the *Elfas* in the north and east of Europe were rumored to be one of those groups of beings with the oneness of consciousness. By whatever name you knew them, they were among the more peaceful of beings, harboring far less animosity towards humans than the troll genes, which he possessed, he thought ironically. They were a race that was at home in nature, quick and fast, beautiful and solitary in their commitment to their land and their people. Fair of skin and known for their near spiritual closeness with the wild.

"I could never stay away from you, Alayna," he said. "Besides, I have not divulged the truth in its entirety to you." She pulled away from his body to get a better look at his face, but kept his hands grasped tightly in her own.

"Nothing you say can matter," she said, "Do not be afraid. I am now different than the girl with whom you fell in love. If you are also different, that is all right. Nothing can change my feelings."

The Collector

He did not know whether her understanding of his feelings was a natural womanly intuition or some enhanced ability given to her by her newfound personhood. He didn't care. She loved him, and he her, and as long as he had that then everything would be fine. He proceeded to tell her the story of his past and the wild genes that flowed in his veins. He described his life-long battle to deny it, and his reluctant and then final surrender to the instincts within himself in a last attempt to save her life. Then he described the freedom he now felt as a result of that acceptance.

Alayna smiled encouragingly, and when he had finished his tale she kissed him thoroughly and passionately. They stayed with lips pressed together for long moments.

When they parted and when Philip finally regained the breath that she had stolen, he smiled with the truest joy he had ever felt and asked, "What now? What will we do?"

Alayna shook her head in surprised disbelief at the turn of events. "My people are everywhere, in this land and many others. I know we would be welcome with them if we so choose," she said, yet her statement held no pressure for Philip to make that choice. They would decide together.

She continued after she saw that he understood that her first commitment was to him, as his was to her now, "I feel the woods pulsing in my blood, the wilderness streaking through my veins."

He took her hand and squeezed in agreement as he felt that similar calling of mountain and forest, water and stone. It was interesting how so many of the non-human races carried this affinity for nature and the wild. As he embraced himself as the half-breed he was, that non-human side of him called out and longed to be wandering where no other soul but his precious Alayna could follow.

"What will you do?" Alayna asked, "What of the Guild?"

Philip struggled within himself. Much of what he had done over the last decades had been right. He had put a stop to violence and captured the vilest of creatures, keeping them from doing harm. The human side of him still longed for that responsibility, to protect those who could not protect themselves. But he was unable with good conscience to convince himself that all of his captures had demonstrated justice, fairness and morality. Just looking at last night and his willingness to put Beathan in

103

the hands of the Guild, a being that had become his friend and proven more worthy and righteous than the senior Guild member who had betrayed him and now lay dead on the floor of this abandoned house, proved it true.

"I don't know," he answered truthfully. "Part of it was—is right, but part of me knows that with the changes of tonight, nothing will ever be the same."

Alayna nodded her understanding and agreement, clasping his hand as she led him from the house. They exited the musty entrance and left the stuffy air behind them, allowing the night's cool breeze to wash over their bodies. It bathed their senses with freedom and beauty, and Philip realized that whether he chose to return to the Guild or not, that decision would not be made tonight. Tonight he and his love would explore true freedom.

Yes, a voice caressed his mind. Startled, he glanced at Alayna, and she grinned in delight. It appeared she was already discovering new talents that she possessed as benefits of the race to which she now belonged. *Tonight we run, for now we roam. The wild awaits.*

Philip unleashed the wilderness he kept contained within himself and reveled in both parts of his personhood, the human and the animal. Yes, tonight indeed was a night for freedom, a night or maybe longer, to run without rules and restrictions.

He could neither speak telepathically as she could, nor read minds so he said aloud, "Where shall we go?"

North her mind pierced his head in beautiful fashion, creating an intimacy he had never known before. Then she furthered it, speaking with her voice not her mind, "Both of our heritages lie in the north. I can feel it." She giggled as if she couldn't wait for the adventure that they both knew awaited them.

They ran north, hand in hand, faster than Philip had ever dreamed he could run. Freedom, and a carefree kind of joy washed over him, just as a wave of stars had bathed the clear night sky above them. Of one thing he was certain—nothing would ever be the same.

About the Author

Mathias Colwell grew up in far Northern California exploring redwood forests and cloudy beaches. He loves God, his family, and friends. Mathias has been a writer for most of his life, drafting his first stories as young as eight years of age. His desire to write fantasy was inspired by such authors as J.R.R. Tolkien, David Eddings and the late Robert Jordan. He is an avid traveler and all-around adventurer, having visited or lived in 27 countries. His travels have led him around the world to five continents including stays in Siberia, Spain, and Chile, and he attributes many of his passions and goals in life to these experiences. In his free time he enjoys reading, outdoor activities such as soccer, snowboarding and water sports. Mathias has a passion for issues pertaining to social justice and human rights and hopes to influence these areas in the future.

Other Works by the author at Melange, Fire and Ice for Young Adults

An Age of Mist